Also available from
Natalie Charles

Archer Cove Series
The Coffee Girl

Harlequin Romantic Suspense

The Seven-Day Target
The Burden of Desire
When No One Is Watching

Natalie Charles

A Sweet Possibility

◆Cranberry Press◆

ISBN-13: 978-0-9862805-3-5

A Sweet Possibility

Cover design: Ebooklaunch.com
Copy Editor: Amanda Sumner

This is a work of fiction. Names, characters, places and incidents are either the product of the author's imagination or are used fictitiously, and any resemblance to actual persons, living or dead, business establishments, events or locales is entirely coincidental.

For my readers, with gratitude

A Sweet
Possibility

CHAPTER ONE

CANDY MADE EVERYTHING better.

Jessie chewed a piece of milk chocolate almond bark and considered the scene around her. Half the contents of her closet were strewn across the unmade double bed, and an old silver thong sandal had somehow worked its way onto the shade on her bedside lamp. In the rush of selecting the appropriate garment, Jessie had blown through what must have been a full decade of her personal fashion statements: sheath dresses with lace overlay, brightly-patterned skirts, shirtdresses in pastel shades, and even a gingham print A-line number that still had the tags. They reminded her of evenings out, and some of them still smelled like her perfume. A sentimental journey, but as Jessie glanced back at the chaos of her bedroom, a pit formed in her stomach. This was not the sign of an ordered life.

She selected the black dress with the built-in sequined belt. It was that or the Amish-style getup with the enormous floral prints on a navy background, and she simply didn't own the orthotic footwear to match. She studied herself in the full-length mirror and wondered when she'd seen this dress last. Perhaps in college, when she'd been going through that clubbing phase? More importantly, why on earth did she still own it? She was grateful to the inner pack rat who developed odd attachments to tacky things. She could neutralize it with a yellow cardigan and call it a day.

Perfect for a Sunday baby shower.

She paired the dress with a small black clutch that contained only the essentials: her driver's license, the credit card that wasn't maxed, a bottle of nail polish in a shade called "Pink Me Up," and a nip of raspberry vodka because...God help her. She'd be seeing her family.

The May morning was unseasonably warm, so Jessie straightened her blonde hair but didn't get too attached to the result. By noon, her hair would be wavy again, giving her a slightly messy look that people might assume she'd intended, given her dress. "Don't give me that look, Travis," she warned the silver fox watching her from behind the front door. "I had an appropriate dress. I just can't zip it."

Some people inherited items of value from their relatives. Her friend Nate, for example, had inherited the little blue cottage she was living in. But when Jessie's Great Aunt Esther died, she'd inherited her taxidermic silver fox. It stood beside the front door, glass eyes patiently staring out at the horizon. She told herself that it was an interest piece and not at all creepy, but she usually hid it when she had company. Prince Travis didn't bother her, but some people simply didn't understand.

She gazed at the light blue dress she'd cast aside on her bed. That had been an unpleasant surprise, not being able to squeeze herself into it this morning. Jessie had been working some long hours at Hedda's Bakery, testing a lot of new chocolate recipes. Tasting was part of the job. She felt around her middle and found a plumpness she hadn't noticed before. Maybe she'd done a little too much tasting. No time to dwell on it, though. She had only twenty minutes to get to Great Barrington.

The drive was easy, the traffic light at this time on a Sunday morning. Jessie followed the highway along the coast from Archer Cove to Great Barrington, rolling down the windows to enjoy the fresh air. Her first day off in weeks, and she was spending it at her cousin Maggie's baby shower. She gritted her teeth. At least her cousin Wren would be there.

She arrived at a massive wrought-iron gate flanked by a thick hedge of arbor vitae. Driving through it was a bit like entering some gaping mouth, following the lengthy driveway like sliding down an esophagus. Then the mansion rose in the distance, a gray Georgian estate. She counted six chimneys and four valets. She pulled her old dark-blue Civic beside a man in black pants, a white dress shirt, and a black vest. He took Jessie's valet key and handed her a pink card with a number 43 on it. "And where's the party?" she asked.

"Which one?" he replied in a bored drawl.

"Maggie Schaeffer's baby shower."

He pointed in the direction of the estate and said, "Follow the signs."

Jessie set off toward the main entrance, and sure enough, in the lobby was a sign with a green arrow that read, "Schaeffer Baby Shower" and pointed to a set of French doors. Green, Jessie supposed, because even though Maggie and Greg knew the gender of the baby, they weren't telling anyone. For the record, this made shopping close to impossible. Jessie had hit no fewer than three baby stores before ultimately settling on a bottle set in primary colors and a yellow blanket.

Through the French doors was a slate patio overlooking an expansive English garden and, in the distance, a cerulean strip of ocean. Jessie stood for a moment to admire the landscaping and to watch a bumblebee climb inside a red tulip. Then her ears were assaulted by a shrill shriek. "There's Jessie!"

She didn't know who said it. It didn't matter. What mattered was that she felt that fake, painful smile spread across her face as she prepared to pretend that she was blissfully happy to be at the baby shower for her third cousin's wife. Her dad's cousin, Louise, who was hosting the shower, came over in a flash of beige. The next thing she knew, her face was being mashed against her ample bosom. "Jessie, sweetheart. Don't you look pretty."

Louise was a lovely woman with a death-grip hug. Jessie mumbled a "thank you" against the silk of her dress.

"You're seated at table seven, with your mom and auntie," Louise said. "You have a lovely time, darling."

On her way to table seven, she passed Maggie, the mother-to-be, who was sitting at a white wrought-iron table decorated with vases of blue and pink lilacs. She was wearing a bubblegum-pink dress that really should have provided more in the way of shoulder straps and breathability in the middle. Unlike Louise, Maggie was very hands-off in her greeting style and preferred to lightly clasp hands and kiss the air beside both cheeks. It would not have surprised Jessie in the least to know that Maggie believed this to be a more dignified, even Continental form of greeting. "Jessie," she sighed in her usual affect, "good to see you, as always."

"You too, Mags. You're glowing."

"Ugh!" She tossed one hand into the air. "I'm swollen all over. Look." She held out one leg and turned it to demonstrate. "It's not even noon, and I have cankles. Doctor says my blood pressure is through the roof. They may have to put me on bed rest, and at that point you may as well throw me off a cliff. What am I going to do on bed rest?"

Jessie smoothed her honey-colored hair reassuringly. "You look beautiful, Mama. Pregnancy suits you."

Maggie's expression took on a wide-eyed look, her blue eyes wild as she leaned in to whisper, "I get so angry sometimes. Is that normal, do you think? I want to smash a chair into the wall."

There was a lengthy pause as Jessie digested this information. Then she tittered a nervous laugh. "I'm sure you're not the first. Maybe it's the blood pressure."

"Well." Maggie righted herself again, a bright smile plastered on her face. "Thanks for coming. I hope you have a great time."

Jessie felt the smile frozen on her face as she walked away. My God, she thought. She's going to kill us all.

"Jess!"

She turned and saw her cousin Wren approaching, carrying a mimosa. Wren looked gorgeous, as always. She'd always been beautiful, with her brown wavy hair, slightly freckled skin, and large, expressive brown eyes, but if it was possible, she'd become even better-looking recently. She was in love, and it suited her. Life was so unfair.

"Thank goodness you're here," Wren gushed. "I thought you were going to stand us up." She kissed her on the cheek. "Nice dress. It's so…fancy. Do you have plans to go out with Quinn afterward?"

"No. The dress I wanted to wear is at the cleaners," Jessie said. "Anyway, I thought about not coming at all. Then I decided I'd just bring alcohol."

Wren wrinkled her nose as Jessie opened her clutch. "Don't even bother with that stuff. The mimosas are flowing freely. This is my second. Here." She handed the flute to Jessie. "You look like you need it more than I do."

Jessie accepted the drink gratefully and took a generous gulp. There she was, on her first day off in

14

weeks, standing in her trashy-looking club dress and yellow cardigan at a baby shower, of all places. She'd never been one to fawn over babies and get excited about weddings. She'd spent most of her time since college working at her uncle's bakery and perfecting her chocolate recipes. Being as busy as she was left her little time to think about settling down.

The large diamond on Wren's left hand caught the sunlight. Last summer Wren, her quiet, mild-mannered cousin, had fallen in love with Hollywood bad boy and Class-A gorgeous man Jax Cosgrove. They'd bought a vineyard overlooking the ocean, and Jax had proposed in the south of France, on the set of one of his films. Wren's own screenplay was set to film in Scotland in a few months — her second film. Their life was glamorous and perfect and down-to-earth all at the same time. "How are things with Jax?" Jessie asked, even though she knew the answer.

Wren's expression brightened. "Great," she beamed. "Wedding plans are going well, and the vineyard is busy. I have your maid of honor dress in the car. You just need to try it on, but it's custom-made, so it should fit like a glove."

Right, the wedding was in August, and Wren's own baby shower was sure to follow. Jessie took another gulp of her mimosa. "How wonderful," she said, with a glance around the patio. "Where are we sitting?"

Wren nodded over her left shoulder. "Over there. They stuck us way in the back. I think I may take it personally."

"I've found it's really the only way to take things."

They were seated at a table with Jessie's mother, Sadie, Wren's mother, Aunt Lilliana, their grandma, and their Great Aunt Doris, all of whom stopped talking as they approached. Never a good sign. Jessie's mom pulled out the chair beside her and patted the seat. "Here, sweetie," she said. "I haven't seen you in a while." Then added, with a level of concern, "How are you doing?"

"I'm not the one you should be worried about," Jessie said. "Maggie has high blood pressure and anger problems."

"She looks like she ate a spare tire," Auntie Lil said before taking a sip of her iced tea.

"Mom, that's not nice." Wren rolled her eyes at Jessie. "She looks adorable."

A smartly-dressed waiter in a silver vest and a bow tie came by with a pitcher of lemon water and poured glasses for Wren and Jessie. The second he left, Sadie leaned over and said earnestly, "How's Quinn?"

Jessie gripped the champagne flute. She had been dating Quinn Rogerson for a few months, and things were *great*. Better than great, because she'd been in love with Quinn since, oh, the first time she'd seen him in high school. He was handsome and smart, and everything she'd ever wanted in a boyfriend. Sure, Quinn bristled at the term "boyfriend." He wanted to keep things more open. All Jessie had to do was to be patient and to show him what a catch she was, and she felt she was making some headway there. But every time her mother asked about Quinn, her voice assumed this desperate note that made Jessie wonder if she viewed Quinn as the Last Hope: either they would marry and have babies, or Jessie was destined live out the rest of her life with ten cats and her taxidermic fox.

"Quinn is doing well," she said. "He's busy. He's working toward partnership," she added, pleased to see Auntie Lil and Grandma nod their heads approvingly. "He's up in August, so. Fingers crossed."

"We all want that to happen," Sadie said gravely. "Partnership will make him a good provider, and men don't usually think about marriage until then."

Jessie glanced around the table and saw more serious nodding. "Jeez, Mom. Is it 1950?"

Wren reached for her empty champagne flute. "You look like you're almost done with your drink. Do you need another one?"

Jessie rubbed at her forehead and closed her eyes. "Yes. Please."

It's not like she was one of those women who was afraid to be alone. After all, she'd gotten this far on her own. Did she think she'd maybe like to have children one day? Sure, why not. But it's not like she was at the point where she actually begrudged other people's happiness. She could sit at that baby shower in her old, slinky, completely inappropriate black dress, next to her blissfully happy cousin, and celebrate someone else's joy without even considering her own life. Like, for example, the fact that she had just turned thirty years old. Or the fact that her perfect boyfriend spent more Friday nights working than with her. No, she could totally ignore all of that and just enjoy the unseasonably warm May morning. She wasn't even bothered by the way her dress was clinging to her back sweat. Life was grand.

Wren came back to the table and set another mimosa in front of her with a sad smile. "Cheers, Jess. It ends at two o'clock."

"Bottoms up." Jessie drank half the flute right away and set the glass down again with a small burp. "You're going to need to keep these coming."

By the time brunch was over and they were playing games to guess the gender and size of Maggie's baby, Jessie was feeling pleasantly tipsy.

Maybe it was horrible that she was getting drunk at a baby shower. She could accept that. It was just that every five minutes, one family member or another was strolling over to the table to ask how Wren's wedding plans were coming along, and then glancing hopefully at Jessie to say something along the lines of, "How about you, honey? Any prospects yet?" As if finding a husband was like panning for gold. When their cousin Melinda walked over — more like sashayed over in her designer clothes and platform heels — Jessie replied that she was taking a break from dating, "Just until the rash on my lady parts clears up."

"People are making conversation," Sadie said as she selected a Parker House roll from the bread basket. "You can't fault them for that."

"They're not making conversation. They're being nosy," Jessie said. "And how come they can't ask me about my business? Am I only defined by my reproductive capabilities?"

She halted her speech when they heard applause and turned to see that the father-to-be, Greg, had entered the patio. He was tall, blond, and self-assured as he gave a charming smile and a wave to the flock of female friends and relatives celebrating his wife. Jessie tilted her head as she studied him, struggling to keep her eyes open. She felt so sleepy. "I never realized how attractive Greg was," she murmured.

"He's your cousin," Wren whispered. "And he's married. With a baby on the way."

"Whatever. Third cousin, anyway." She took another gulp of her drink.

"It's weird all the same."

Jessie tapped her glass with her fingernail. "Wren? I'm empty."

Wren patiently moved the glass out of reach. "I think you've had enough. You're not driving, by the way."

"I'll sober up in time," Jessie said, but didn't object when Wren lifted her keys from her clutch. "The valet has my car key. You're just locking me out of my house. Oh, fine. You want me to get a ride?" She sighed and took out her cell phone to text Quinn. "There. All set."

"Good," Wren said.

"Oh look. It's time for presents." Aunt Doris groaned and sat back in her chair.

"Does this make you regret not having children?" Sadie asked. Doris had never married, though rumor had it she'd received several proposals.

She sputtered her lips. "That's like asking someone if they regret not being whipped."

"Some people like being whipped," Jessie said matter-of-factly and reached for Wren's mimosa, figuring what was the harm? She wasn't driving. Wren slapped her hand away. "It's a big thing. Spankings."

"For children?" Auntie Lil asked.

"No, Mom," Wren said. "She means kink. You know, handcuffs and chains."

Auntie Lil's cheeks turned pink and she sat rigidly in her chair, her eyes fixed on Maggie and Greg, who were pulling baby shampoo out of a small bag and gasping, "Thank you."

"I've seen that brand before," Auntie Lil said. "Is that organic?"

"They're overselling the gratitude," Jessie muttered.

"Don't change the subject, you two," Doris said. "This shower was just getting interesting."

They sat in virtual silence — aside from the obligatory *ooh*s and *ahh*s — as Maggie opened her gifts. A handmade baby quilt. Too many yellow and green onesies to count. A baby monitor with a built-in video camera. Knickknacks that Jessie didn't see the point of. The sun was blaring by then, and she was sweltering in the shade of the umbrella. Even if her other dresses didn't fit, Jessie regretted not wearing something more breathable.

After they'd opened a veritable mountain of baby gifts, Maggie rose and gave a polite and nearly heartwarming speech thanking everyone for their generosity. Then Louise announced that Maggie and Greg should go cut their shower cake, and Jessie mumbled, "At least there's dessert. That quiche didn't sit well with me."

They cut the cake together, their hands overlapping on the knife, and the crowd sighed in approval. Then Greg ran his finger along the side of the knife to gather a clump of frosting, which he then dotted on Maggie's nose.

That's about the time all hell broke loose.

Maggie's face turned a deep red. "Do you think that's funny? To put frosting on my face at my baby shower?"

A bewildered Greg looked at his wife, terror creeping across his handsome features. "I don't — it was a joke. I didn't mean —"

"Like hell you didn't!" Maggie grabbed a fistful of cake and mashed it into his face. "How do you like it?"

Louise hurled herself between them, but Maggie simply leaned back and gave her a solid punch to the jaw. Pandemonium ensued, as a herd of women in pastel brunch attire swarmed the situation.

"Leave me alone! Back off!" Maggie was taking clumps of cake and hurling them, baseball-style, at anyone who came near.

"Oh." Jessie sat back in her chair, suddenly feeling more awake. "Oh, this is good."

"We should intervene or something," Auntie Lil said, taking a sip of her iced tea. "I mean, someone should stop this."

"And how do you think we should do that?" Sadie said as a lump of cake splattered only inches from her seat.

"Turn a garden hose on her," Grandma replied. "They must have a garden hose."

"Please don't." Jessie sighed. "This is amazing. I wish I'd brought popcorn."

It turned out that the garden hose was not necessary after all, and once the staff intervened, Maggie calmed herself enough to stop throwing cake. A moment or two passed. Then, all at once, she glanced around at her guests, who were covered in cake and frosting, and burst into tears. "I'm sorry. I'm so sorry."

Silence followed. A long, awkward silence. Louise stumbled to the center of the patio, a glass of iced tea pressed against the left side of her jaw. "I think that's all, everyone. Thank you for coming."

Then she started sobbing, too, and Greg froze, looking like he didn't know who to comfort first. This only made Maggie cry harder, and she stood alone with her frosting-covered hands over her face, her pink dress smeared with cake innards and — strawberries? Yes, strawberries. It was a fruit cake. Just as well it was ruined.

Later on, Jessie told herself that she hadn't had a choice. Everyone was just sitting and staring at Maggie and Greg and Louise, and people were crying, and the guests were coated in frosting and who knew what else.

The waitstaff was rushing to clean up broken ceramics and glass on the patio. Maggie had punched her mother-in-law on the jaw, for God's sake. Someone had to do something, and Jessie fortunately had champagne and orange juice running through her veins, which dulled any inclination for second thoughts.

"Ahem." She clinked the side of her water glass with her fork and rose. "Could I have everyone's attention, please?"

"Saint Michael on a pony. What are you doing, Jessica?" Sadie hid her face behind a napkin.

"Attention, please." Slowly eyes turned, and that's when Jessie realized she had no idea what to say. "Right. I, uh...let's end this thing on a good note, okay? Because aside from a little blip in the last ten minutes, this was a lovely baby shower. To the extent these things can be enjoyable at all."

She felt every pair of eyes on her as she spoke — more like, as she fumbled to grasp the thoughts randomly firing through her mind. And every set of eyes was looking at her like *she* was the troublemaker. Except for Wren, who was nodding at every word with rapt attention. "Hear, hear," Wren said. "This was a great shower. Historic."

"Memorable," Jessie agreed. "And that's because Maggie and Greg are special people. Mags, you're this ridiculously talented photographer. You've traveled all over the world, and your work has been displayed in magazines and museums, right? Museums, people. Galleries. She's passionate, and she's an artist, and I know

23

she's so excited about this baby. I for one am looking forward to seeing how she photographs the little...person." She took a sip of her water and continued. "I'm not going to talk about the cake incident, because you know what? People handle pregnancy differently, and she —" She pointed to Maggie. "She's an angry preggo, and I'm afraid she'll break my face if I do that. Am I right, Mags? You don't need to answer, I already know it's true. It's not your fault. It's like your cankles. You can blame it all on the little parasite in your uterus."

"Tread lightly," Sadie said through a frozen smile, but Jessie continued, undeterred.

"Anyway, you're great, Mags. I love you. We all love you, even when you're pregnant. And we love that little bun in your oven, whatever it is. Greg, you're great, too, but maybe next time don't put frosting on your pregnant wife's face. And Louise, this was a beautiful shower that no one is going to forget. The best part is that most of us get to wear our dessert home." She raised her water glass. "Cheers."

Silence. At first Jessie thought that she'd really gone and done it now, and she was watching Maggie's face to see whether she was going to hurl that platter of cookies in her direction, but Maggie broke into a big smile. Then she grabbed her impressive stomach and started laughing. Greg's shoulders relaxed and he started laughing, too, and pretty soon the tension on the patio dissolved as they all caught on. Jessie chuckled too, even though she wasn't sure what the joke was.

Still, the party was clearly over, and the guests pushed in their chairs, helped clean up the cake, and made their way out of the garden. Maggie gave Jessie a real kiss on the cheek this time — a greasy one that made her wipe her face. "Jess," she giggled. "How much did you drink?"

She glanced around. "Is it that obvious?"

"A little bit. I hope you're not driving."

"No way. I promise. You take care of yourself."

"I will."

She headed inside and took a quick glance around the lobby. There, on the far end by the entry doors, was Quinn. He was consumed by something on his cell phone, and he stared down at the screen, not noticing that she was approaching. Jessie smiled to herself. He really was so handsome. She had dreamed of dating him in high school, when he was captain of the varsity football team. Sometimes she had to pinch herself. *This was her life.* "Hey, stranger," she cooed. "You got my text."

He looked up then and smiled. "Hey, Jess." He ran his gaze over her figure. "Why are you dressed like that?"

She stopped and looked down. "It's a baby shower."

Quinn tucked his phone into his back pocket and sighed. "You got drunk at a baby shower."

"I had a few mimosas. It's my first day off in weeks, and I think I'm feeling it more because I'm slightly dehydrated, and —"

"It's okay. No harm done. Look, I have to get to work," he said. "It's an emergency."

"An emergency? I thought we were going to spend some time together today." She crossed her arms, feeling pouty. "You're a lawyer. You don't work triage."

"I don't make fun of your pastries, Jess." He leaned over and kissed her chastely on the forehead. "I'm sorry, hon. We have that dinner party later, remember? You should go home and...sober up."

"Funny. I'm not *that* bad off." Not so bad that she didn't know a blow-off when she heard it. "So, fine. Let's get going."

He avoided her gaze and turned back to his cell phone. "Actually, Nate's bringing you home. I came with him. Someone had to drive your car." Quinn glanced over his shoulder. "Here he is."

On cue, Nate Lancaster walked through the doorway, his sandy brown hair looking just slightly messy. He was broad-shouldered and lean, with a strong jawline and deep-set green eyes. He walked in like he owned the place, trailing confidence. Jessie tried not to make a face. If Quinn saw that, he'd be upset, because he and Nate were best buds. Jessie liked Nate, too. They'd always been close, and he was the one who'd introduced her to Quinn. Nate was easy to like — except when he saw an opportunity to tease her. Then he was *merciless*.

She braced herself.

Nate looked Jessie up and down, making no effort to hide his appraisal. "What the hell happened to you?"

"Ugh." She turned back to Quinn and prepared one last plea. "What if Nate drives my car and I get a ride with you?"

26

"That doesn't make sense, babe. I promise I'll see you later, all right? The dinner is very important."

Of course it was, she thought. Because it was related to work, and work was very important to Quinn. She pressed her lips together but didn't say anything more. "I'll be ready at six."

"Wren gave me your keys," Nate said brightly, spinning her keyring on his finger. "Looks like I get to drive Old Cobalt."

Jessie shot him her best drop-dead stare. "My car isn't that old. And you don't get to make fun of it."

"I'm not making fun. I like antiques."

"All right, kids," Quinn said. "You run along. The adults have to get to work." He leaned over and gave Jessie a kiss on the cheek. "Be nice to my friend."

"Me?" She gasped and pointed to Nate. "He's the one who called my car an antique!"

"I'm leaving. I'll pick you up at six."

Quinn's black BMW convertible was double-parked at the entrance, so he gave a quick wave before climbing inside and speeding away. Jessie watched the dust rising behind his car for several moments before she heard Nate clear his throat beside her. She started. "What?"

He gestured to the man in the vest waiting expectantly. "Do you have a valet ticket?"

"Oh," she blinked. "Sorry."

She opened her clutch to search for it, and Nate chuckled. "Did you pack that vodka for the baby shower? Or is that left over from church?"

Jessie's cheeks grew warm, but she lifted her ticket and handed it to the valet, all business. "Not your concern."

"Uh huh." He shoved his hands into the pockets of his jeans and rolled back on his heels, clearly delighted with his discovery. "That's what I thought. Tell me the truth: that's a novice habit you're wearing, isn't it? I can tell by the sequined belt. Does Quinn know you're taking a vow of chastity?"

It was fair punishment, she supposed. Get drunk at a baby shower, suffer a ride home with Nate at his finest. But just then she was starting to feel dizzy, and between his comments and the glare off the Civic as the valet pulled it up...She closed her eyes. "Just...can I have some quiet? Just for a few minutes?"

"You're the boss," Nate said as he opened the passenger-side door and slipped a few bills into the valet's hand. "Your chariot awaits, madame."

"Gosh, Nate. And to think you had nothing better to do this morning."

"Lucky for you, sunshine."

As she took a seat, he shut the door, narrowly missing her ankle. Jessie leaned her head back against the headrest and stared out the window. She swore she would never touch a mimosa again.

CHAPTER TWO

THE VALETS HAD blasted the air conditioner before returning the Civic, but the air inside the car was still stale and hot. Nate felt like he was breathing through a wet towel. Jessie always drove with the windows down, which Nate took as evidence that the air conditioner didn't work at all. Ever since she'd found that mouse nest in her engine, she'd claimed that "the works" in the old car hadn't been the same. He speculated that the failing "works" had less to do with a mouse nest and more to do with the fact that the car had been kicking around since the Paleolithic era.

He attempted to squeeze himself into the driver's seat. Failed. "Have you been transporting elephants in the backseat? Why do you drive so close to the steering wheel?"

"Just move the seat back," she said, staring straight ahead. "The lever's in front."

"Still. It's not safe. You could get killed by an airbag."

"I'll take that under advisement, thank you. Oh, and don't turn on the radio while the car is going or the engine will stall. And you can't run the air conditioner and the windshield wipers at the same time."

He paused. "You sure this car is safe?"

"Totally safe. You just can't do those things."

He adjusted his seat back, eyeing his companion sidelong. Jessie had a cloud following her. Nate could tell by her sullen expression as she fastened her seatbelt. He'd always imagined baby showers to be torturous events, but weren't women supposed to like them? Damned if he'd ever understand any of it. "Are you going to throw up?" he asked as he fastened his own seatbelt. "I can roll down your window and you can just stick your head out, real classy-like. Unless you keep bags in here for these occasions."

Jessie waved a hand at him. "I only had three mimosas. Maybe five."

"Whatever. It's not my upholstery." Nate tilted the rearview mirror. "You don't look well."

"Wow, thanks a lot." She turned to stare at him with wide eyes. "You know, that's a rude thing to say to someone."

"I meant, you look upset."

"Oh." She deflated, then leaned back, resting her hands over her stomach as she seemed to puzzle over the statement. "I guess I'm just thinking about things." She paused. "I have cake on my shoes." She didn't bother to wipe it off.

"Like I said, it's not my upholstery."

He pulled out of the parking lot and followed a gravel drive back to the main road. He hadn't been to Breaker House in ages. For some reason, he'd thought it was closed. It was a stuffy place that seemed to have been built with proms and pretenses in mind, and people had given him funny looks when he'd entered wearing jeans. He glanced over at Jessie and smiled. He had no idea why she had cake all over her, or why she was wearing that clubbing dress, but he sort of loved that she'd passed through Breaker House like she'd just wandered in from spring break. But to be honest, he sort of loved everything about her. He had for as long as he could remember.

She shifted in her seat, and Nate's attention was brought back to the road. "At least you had fun."

Jessie snorted. "Fun? No, I don't think I had fun. It was all a little bit horrible. Although the cake fight was great." She sighed and stared straight ahead. "But I was looking at Maggie — that's my cousin. Third cousin's wife, actually. Third-cousin-in-law? Anyway, she's having this baby, and that's amazing. And she also has this glamorous job and a solid marriage. Well, aside from the fruit cake," she added, but Nate didn't know what that meant. "And then Wren's career has completely taken off and she's writing and traveling the world with Jax, who adores her." She stopped. "I'm talking too much. I do that sometimes when I drink."

"That's okay, I'm only half-listening." He counted it as a victory when she forced a small laugh. Encouraged, he added, "You sound discontented."

"That's a good word for it, yes. Discontented. I'm discontented. First, because what about *my* dreams? I've always wanted to own my own chocolate shop, and here I am, still working at Hedda's."

Jessie's uncle owned Hedda's Bakery, and Jessie had worked there for years. When Nate first met her in high school, she was living with her uncle and her cousin Wren in the apartment above the bakery. She didn't talk much about her own parents, but he'd gathered they had moved to Europe for a few years and wanted Jessie to stay behind. She'd always seemed fine with it, and didn't mention it much. It wasn't like it had scarred her for life.

If anything, living with her uncle seemed to give Jessie direction. She was a brilliant baker, and in recent years she'd been experimenting with her own line of chocolates, which she'd set out in a brand-new display case in the bakery. "I always thought your chocolates were selling well," he said.

She gave a halfhearted shrug and made a noise that sounded like, "Meh."

"It takes a lot to build a business. Sometimes it's painful."

He knew that all too well. Nate was a personal trainer who'd built his client list over a number of years, taking on odd jobs when business was slow. He'd finally broken past that point, and business was booming. He was almost having trouble fitting in all his client appointments, and he'd started to consider what the next move would be. "It will happen," he concluded. He liked to put an end to problems, wrap things up and tie a bow on them — figuratively speaking, of course.

"Not as long as I'm in Hedda's," she said. "I need my own space. Somewhere to grow and expand. I want to feel proud of where I am."

He watched her out of the corner of his eye as he pulled to a stop at an intersection. "You got all of that from a baby shower? What, did they have a motivational speaker there?"

"I took away two things," she said. "One, I'm not where I want to be professionally. Second, I'm not where I want to be personally." She tugged at the ends of her blonde hair. "All of these people close to me are getting married and having babies. It never bothered me before. I'd think, well, I'm a feminist. Fish on bicycles and whatnot. I had my career, and I didn't need to get married. Except I sort of want that. The whole thing."

He studied her as they waited for the light to change. "What whole thing, Jess?"

Part of him didn't want to know, because she was dating Quinn. The other part of him held onto hope that today would be the day she'd come to her senses and give him a chance. Maybe they wanted the same whole thing.

"You know, the white picket fence. The pillow fights. The boring Saturday nights on the couch. Stability and ugly flannel sheets. Children and a dog and Christmas morning." She counted the items on her fingers. "I don't need them, but I want them. The American dream." She

33

leaned her head against the window. "I don't know why I'm telling you this. Like you even care. I'm going to have to talk to Quinn tonight."

Nate's stomach dropped. What did he expect, anyway? If she wanted a picket fence and a husband, Quinn was the logical choice. He was almost partner at his firm, so he'd have the financial means to make it happen. Nate may have taught the uber-wealthy how to do squat thrusts and dead lifts and compete in marathons, but that was a far cry from being one of them. Quinn, on the other hand, was approaching their ranks.

But Quinn didn't want a commitment, and he'd said that more than once. To him, Jessie was a friend with benefits — just someone to pass the time with. But try telling her that, when her feelings so obviously went deeper.

He took a deep breath. "You know that a new space just opened up in Archer Cove, right? It's only a few blocks from Hedda's. The Dinardo Deli space."

"What?" Her jaw dropped. "Wait. Shut the front door! When did that happen?"

The store had been vacant for months, and lots of people in town had been speculating about what would fill it. Nate played apologetic. "Oh, I'm sorry. I didn't mean to be useful to you. Did you still want that quiet you asked for?"

"Nate, come on. Tell me about it."

He suppressed a grin. It was kind of hot when she begged for things. "I just saw a "For Rent" sign this morning." He hesitated. "Do you want to stop by, or do you need to sleep it off first?"

"Stop by, for sure! I told you, I only had three mimosas." She reached over and pinched his arm. "Jeez, aren't you supposed to have a layer of fat here? What am I supposed to pinch?"

"I'm in training. I have a marathon in the fall."

"Ugh. Running." She rolled her eyes. "*Miserable.*"

They had known each other since high school, and in all that time, Nate had been running long distances and Jessie had been wrinkling her nose at it. He went to college on a track scholarship, and he couldn't imagine giving up running now, after all these years. It was his time alone with his thoughts. When he met with new clients, they often asked him how they were supposed to fit exercise into their busy daily schedules, and he'd explain that if they stuck with it long enough, their lives would simply make room.

"It's not that bad," he said. "You should try it. You might like it."

"What, running? The horrors. Not unless a tiger is chasing me."

"I can roar, you know. Mrs. Burgess demands it."

Jessie groaned. "I'll bet she does. Oh my gosh, you should date Mrs. Burgess. Wouldn't that be funny?"

Nate cursed silently. Sometimes he wondered if he and Jessie actually spoke the same language. If they did, he must be using it wrong, because she so clearly missed everything he thought he was saying to her.

Date Claire Burgess? In a word, no. Was she attractive? Sure. But she was also a headache and a diva, and attractive wore off quickly. And oh, by the way, he happened to be in love with the girl sitting right beside him. You know, the one he rearranged his entire schedule for because she got wasted at a Sunday morning baby shower. The one who happened to be sort-of dating his best friend, which made things just a little awkward. Okay, a lot awkward. Terrible, really. His best friend on the planet was dating the girl of Nate's dreams, and he couldn't bring himself to even think about what that actually entailed. Better not to think about them dating at all.

"Why would I date Mrs. Burgess?" He didn't mean to sound weary, but he sure felt it just then.

"You would date Mrs. Burgess," Jessie explained in her overly patient tone, "because then we could throw amazing parties. Think about it. We could do a party for every season, and in the summer we'd have an intimate gathering on her yacht. What's she call it?"

"The *Magpie*."

Jessie's mouth dropped. "No, she doesn't! Well, that would have to be renamed. I'm not throwing a summer solstice party on a boat called The *Magpie*."

"You want to talk about horrors," he deadpanned.

They were only a block from Maple Street, where Dinardo's Deli used to be. Jessie was considering her fingernails, which she'd painted a bright pink. "You know about structural things, right? I mean, you can tell me if this space is good to rent?"

"I can give you the basics."

She nodded and returned her hands to her lap, apparently satisfied with that answer. Nate liked to think he was good for something other than collecting her rent checks. Which he hated to do. It was weird to be a landlord to the girl of his dreams. He'd been all set to let Jessie live in that cottage for nothing until she'd insisted on paying him rent. It barely covered the property taxes. But he knew Jessie. *Really* knew her, because her life was one giant open book. He knew that she could barely rub two pennies together, between working at a little bakery and investing just about everything she made into her chocolate business. If he hadn't offered her the cottage, she never would've been able to afford to move out of the apartment above the bakery. She deserved a nicer space than that.

"And here we are!"

They came to a stop in front of the brick facade and empty storefront where Dinardo's Deli used to be. The place had been in business for decades. It was a convenient stop before tourists hit the beaches, or a quick place to grab a bite if you worked in town. He remembered standing in line here with his mom when he was a kid to buy cold cuts, or saving his allowance to buy a novelty ice cream bar from the freezer. When George Dinardo retired, he took the energy of the place with him. Now it was only an empty space with some countertops.

"I'm nervous," she whispered, clutching his forearm.

Early on, he'd learned that Jessie was the affectionate, touchy type. At first he'd allowed himself to believe it was personal and that she was attracted to him. But no, she was like that with all of her friends, and sometimes with virtual strangers. The challenge for him was figuring out where he could touch her back in a way that was friendly, considering that left to his own instincts, he'd pull her into his arms every time she brushed his shoulder or playfully wrapped an arm around his waist in a half-hug. The gentle contact that would have once thrilled him felt increasingly like a turn of the screw.

He stiffly patted her shoulder. "Buck up, buttercup. If it's not this space, another one will come along."

But they both knew that Archer Cove was pretty much built-out and that commercial space was in short supply. He'd thought of opening his own place from time to time: a gym that would allow clients to visit him rather than making so many house calls. He could get better equipment and grow his client list, maybe even hire some staff. Try finding a space that made sense and was ready to go for that purpose, though. Nate didn't exactly relish the idea of a rehab, and the spots he'd seen in Great Barrington were...yeesh. Pricey.

Locals referred to this area of Archer Cove as the "downtown," which was flat-out wishful thinking. The area was quaint, with one- and two-story buildings occupied by small-town shops. The florist. The used bookstore. The art gallery. The specialty coffee roaster, the small general store and souvenir shop. In the summer, a constant stream of beachgoers kept the shops busy, but from what he'd heard from the proprietors, business was steady year-round. Dinardo's Deli sat on the corner of

Yardley Avenue like a gatekeeper to the entire area. When real estate was all about location, location, location, this was a desirable spot.

As they peered through the dust-covered windows, Jessie bounced in place on her toes and said, "There's someone in there. I wonder if it's the real estate agent. Could be someone interested in renting."

The man she'd pointed to had a small silver mustache and was dressed for the golf course in khaki pants and a red-collared shirt. Not that Nate was one to judge, since he was dressed for sitting around on the couch. And Jessie may have been cake-splattered, but she still managed to look presentable. She always looked cute.

She knocked on the glass door and waited, bobbing nervously as the man approached and cracked the door.

"Yes, can I help you?" He was carrying a clipboard and everything.

"We were wondering if we could see the space? Are you the listing agent?"

"Yes, I just finished showing the place. I'm Dean."

"Jessie." They shook hands. "And this is Nate. My...driver."

He shot her a look as he shook hands with Dean. "You're the listing agent?"

"I am, and I have to warn you, I've had a lot of interest in this space."

Of course he had, Nate thought drily. No one ever sold anything by telling a potential buyer that no one else wanted it. But Jessie wrung her hands nervously as Dean opened the door.

Funny how old, familiar spaces look different when they're empty. He must've been to Dinardo's several hundred times, but with the space cleared out like this, he saw it anew. It was a corner space with large windows on two walls. There was a wall and a swinging door behind the counter that led to the kitchen, but all of that could easily be removed to create an open plan. The gray tile was tired-looking, chipped in the corners or cracked. He'd never noticed before, when there was inventory and furniture to distract from flaws.

Jessie must have had a similar thought because she said, "I could clear out the counters and displays, right?"

"You'll have a lot of flexibility with the interior," Dean said. "These fixtures are going to be removed before a tenant takes the space."

Jessie craned her neck as she walked around, studying the gray tiles and running her fingertips along the drywall. "It needs some work," Nate said. "More than fresh paint."

"The tenant is responsible for the interior," Dean replied.

"The ceiling needs to be patched and repainted," he said. "That water spot doesn't look good. It may need a new roof."

Jessie stopped in place to stare at the brownish spot on the ceiling. "The landlord will pay for that, right?"

"That may be old," Dean said. "But yes, exterior maintenance is the landlord's responsibility. That will be in the lease."

They walked through the kitchen. White tile, pretty good condition, except Dinardo's had tiled around their now-missing appliances, leaving square holes on the floor. "You'd have to retile," Nate said, though he didn't really have to.

Jessie groaned softly. "I have to retile this whole space? How much will that cost?"

"Depends who you talk to and what kind of tile you choose. I know a few people who could price out the job for you."

He was trying to be helpful — wasn't that why she'd brought him here? Her brow furrowed, and her lips did that little pouting thing they did when she was thinking about something. Adorable. "You could get a small business loan," he offered. "That could help you get established."

"Maybe." He could practically see her crunching the numbers right there. "Dean, what's the rent?"

He consulted his clipboard. Apparently it wasn't simply for show. "They're asking thirty dollars a square foot. That's annual. Plus utilities. And if property taxes increase, the tenant is responsible to pay the difference." He slipped the clipboard under his arm.

Was that what commercial properties in Archer Cove were going for these days? Nate glanced at Jessie. The blood had drained from her face. He cleared his throat. "Thirty dollars a square foot? You'll never rent this space for that much."

It was obvious that all the scoffing in the world wasn't going to move Dean, who shrugged and said, "It's not negotiable, I'm afraid."

Jessie looked up at Nate, her blue eyes enormous. And devastated. It hit him square in the gut. "Let's think about it, okay, Jess? I don't like those spots on the ceiling or that kitchen. That other place we looked at was much more reasonable."

He wrapped an arm lightly around her shoulders and attempted to lead her out the door. She shuffled along reluctantly. "What other space?" she said.

"You know, that *other* space," Nate said as he squeezed her upper arm, hoping she'd play along. He was trying to make himself useful here, damn it.

"Oh, right. That space." Jessie nodded. "That was great. Much less expensive, too," she added loudly.

Dean shrugged. "It sounds like you have your heart set on the other location." He shut the door behind them and locked it. "You'll keep me posted if you change your mind."

Nate managed to get Jessie across the road and out of earshot before she shrieked, "Thirty dollars a square foot? Is that even *legal* to charge that much?"

"Hey. Don't get discouraged. Some other space will open up. You just have to keep looking until it does. This is just the first try."

She nodded silently, and they walked to the car without talking. There was no need. He'd seen the look on her face, and he was racking his brain, trying to figure out how to make it better. If he could somehow fix this for her, then maybe she'd be happier. If he could ask around in Great Barrington, maybe one of his clients —

"It would've been so perfect." She swiped her fingers across her cheeks as they reached the car. "The kitchen was exactly right. But I guess it's just not meant to be."

They climbed into the blue Civic and continued down the road to Jessie's place in silence. When he pulled the car in front of her cottage, Jessie hesitated before exiting the car. "I shouldn't have made you drive me to look at a storefront. I'm not even ready to open my own place. Blame it on the mimosas."

"Those must have been some mimosas."

"I can't believe I just looked at a space like this. Look at me!" She covered her face with her hands. "My God. Does my breath smell like alcohol?"

She leaned across the console, her lips parted, her breath tickling his cheek. Nate swallowed and turned away. "It doesn't," he said.

It was the truth. She smelled like flowers, not booze.

"Thank goodness." She grabbed her bag and opened the door. "Thanks for the ride. Oh! Is that the dress?" She reached into the backseat and found a white zippered garment bag. "My maid of honor dress, for Wren's wedding. She must've put it in here after the shower. Anyway, I feel like I should give you a ride home. I mean, in a few hours."

"It's only a short walk." He handed her the keys. "Promise me you're staying here for a while."

"Promise."

Her smile stirred something inside of him. A warmth followed by a singe of frustration, because sometimes he wondered why he wasted his time thinking about the girl who was dating his best friend. He should reevaluate his life, too. Maybe move on from Jessie Mallory, once and for all.

Yeah, fat chance.

But on the walk home, wandering beside the pastel-colored picket fences, he thought about the run-down Dinardo space, and how if he could just knock down some of those walls, he'd be able to fit plenty of athletic equipment, and how the windows on the sides could be opened for ventilation. Yes, the space could be perfect for a gym. Not at that price, but prices could be negotiated. Even when someone said they couldn't.

The more he thought about it, the more his resolve strengthened. It was time for him to make some changes in his life, too. Time to do something to give him a chance to succeed, to show that he wasn't just some rudderless guy enjoying an extended adolescence. Jessie responded to success — look at how much she adored Quinn.

His pace quickened. Maybe he was a has-been in some ways. A former track star, a failed professional runner. But that didn't mean he couldn't really make something of himself. He needed some focus, that was all.

Jessie could be that focus. It was time for him to show her who he was. He opened up his cell phone and dialed the number for George Dinardo. When the call went to voicemail, he took a deep breath. "Mr. Dinardo? This is Nate Lancaster. I want to talk with you about that space you have for rent."

CHAPTER THREE

THE COTTAGE WAS small but cheerful, with three large windows that faced the ocean and wispy white curtains that billowed gently against any breeze that passed through. The furnishings were simple: her sitting area consisted of a sofa, an easy chair, and a small oval coffee table — none of which matched, giving the home a cozy, unpretentious feel. When she had someone over, Jessie pulled out the small table and chair set that were normally pushed against the wall. Otherwise, Jessie ate her meals while standing at the kitchen counter or reading on the couch. She didn't see the need to set a table for one. Most of the walls were painted beige, which really bummed her out because...*beige*. Who wanted to stare at beige walls? She'd asked Nate if she could paint them a tasteful shade of purple, and he'd nearly choked at the suggestion. If he saw a few samples, he might come around. In the meantime, she hoped he wouldn't go into the bathroom, which she'd painted a lovely periwinkle a few weeks ago on her day off. She had eight hundred square feet of living space. She might as well have a *little* color.

She took a nap on the sofa and felt much better after that. Then she spent the afternoon tidying up. The weeks got so busy, and the cottage didn't have room enough to forgive clutter. She'd just finished when she glanced at the clock. Time to get ready.

Archer Cove was a little haven in Connecticut, nestled in close proximity to New York but feeling worlds away. In short, it was not the place in which one expected to find a high-powered law firm, but Emerson & Parker came pretty darn close to just that. With large offices in Boston, New York, and Washington, DC, Emerson & Parker was developing a strong regional presence, and rumor had it that the partnership had national ambitions. All of which only served to make Jessie's palms clammy as she thought about rubbing elbows with Quinn's colleagues and bosses that evening.

At least Jessie's cocktail dress still fit, even if it was a little more snug around the waist than she'd like. Her mother's voice rang in her ears: *Thank heavens for small mercies.* Her mother was always thanking heaven for something or other, which was weird since she'd always been a little vague about her actual religious beliefs.

The fabric of the dress was chartreuse and slightly elastic. She pulled at it and hoped the fibers would relax just a little to give her some breathing room. After a minute or so of progressively violent tugging, Jessie conceded defeat. Also, this shade of green had looked nicer on the mannequin. Hopefully it was the lighting.

"What do you think, Travis?" she said, glancing over her shoulder. "I'm taking risks with my wardrobe, and color is in this spring."

Now she was talking to herself again. That seemed to be the natural progression of things: live alone, toil in solitude, and end up talking to yourself a lot. "I get out sometimes, Travis. I just saw Nate. Quinn's friend. You know, the runner? I swear I'm not saying that to make you feel bad, poor thing. I know your feet are glued in place."

She pressed her lips together and decided that maybe it was time to get a cat, or at least a potted fern. Something alive.

Aside from the dress — which was really only ugly under this lighting, she concluded — Jessie decided she looked great. Her skin was glowing, and her blonde hair was...well, as compliant as it could ever be. She'd curled it and hairsprayed it, and it was stiff but still curly. *Saint Mary on a pogo stick! Thank heavens!*

Jessie rubbed her temples. This was what she got from even small doses of her parents, and she'd be hearing her mom's voice for days.

She noticed Quinn's car pull up in front right before he lightly tapped his horn. Man, did that ice her cupcakes when he did that. But she pulled on a smile as she locked the door behind her and ambled down the front walkway, teetering slightly in her heels.

Quinn rolled down the passenger-side window of his BMW. "You're going to be cold in that. The cocktail party's outside."

She glanced down at her cap sleeves. "I'll be fine," she said, but wasn't convinced when a breeze brushed past her bare legs. "Okay, hold on and I'll grab a shawl."

A few minutes later, Jessie re-emerged from her cottage wrapped in a white silk shawl that wasn't going to offer much in the way of protection from the evening chill. But it was something. She climbed into the passenger seat and brushed her lips against Quinn's cheek. "You look nice," she said.

"You too. New dress?"

"Uh huh. Do you like it?"

"Yes. I do like it. It's very nice."

Jessie bit her lip. Quinn was lying. She could tell by the way he'd flatly repeated her question and then added an extra, insincere compliment for emphasis. Her dress was hideous: confirmed. "You know, it is cooler than I thought," she said. "Maybe I should change —"

"You'll be fine. Come on. We're going to be late." He shifted the car into gear and sped away from the curb, knocking Jessie back into her seat.

"Hey." She snapped her seatbelt in place and managed to right herself before he swerved around the corner. "I was ready on time."

Quinn glanced over, looking mildly apologetic. "It's my fault, hon. I was working on that new file Walter gave me." He reached up to scratch at his freshly-shaven cheek. "I haven't been taking a lunch in weeks. You don't even know, Jess."

Her spine stiffened. She thought she *did* know, considering she hadn't seen him or spent any significant amount of time with him for, oh, three weeks now. She laced her fingers with his. "You've been working so hard. I miss you."

Quinn glanced at her from the corner of his eye. "I'm trying to set up my future here. I know you understand." He pulled his hand away from hers to shift gears again.

They were going to the Marina in Spencer. Wills Parker owned a massive yacht and was entitled to equally massive tax benefits if he used it for business entertainment purposes for a certain number of days out of the year. This explained his annual client cruise to Bermuda, for instance. And his partnership cruise through the British Virgin Islands. In addition, he routinely invited the Archer Cove office of Emerson & Parker to yacht parties during the warmer months. Sunday night events were atypical, but Mrs. Parker had celebrated her birthday the night before. Oddly enough, she hadn't wanted to share the spotlight with her husband's employees.

This particular event was intended to celebrate the end of another successful tax season. From what Jessie could gather from hearing Quinn's tales, it was all just an excuse to run an obscene tab of seafood and booze. Associates ended up jumping off the dock by the end of the night or making babies in bathrooms, that kind of thing. It was not her scene or Quinn's, but it was darn

50

important for her to make a good impression if she was going to one day be an Emerson & Parker wife.

Oh, to be an Emerson & Parker wife. This was no small thing. Emerson & Parker wives were graceful and stylish. They maintained a neat home and held dinner parties — Quinn and Jessie had been to a few. They had manicures and — Jessie imagined — creatively landscaped bikini regions. They lunched with each other and usually had help with the children, because they were more than stay-at-home-mothers and wives. They were instrumental in assisting their husbands to rise at the firm.

Partner, Quinn had once explained, was only the first step. There were levels of partners, and perception was everything. If Walter Emerson's wife didn't like another partner's wife, then that partner wasn't going to advance. Everyone knew that. From what Jessie could gather, there was also an unwritten handbook on the qualities that made an Emerson & Parker wife successful. So far, she'd noted that their hair was long and never gray — unless they were over sixty. Their perfume was designer. At least, they smelled expensive. Jessie's underarms grew damp just thinking about seeing them that night, and then they grew damper still as she worried about how all of this anxiety might make her stink. Her performance at the baby shower that morning had been unbecoming, and would not have earned her an invitation to lunch at the country club with the other E&P wives.

She thought back to her mother's hopeful inquiry that morning, when she'd asked about Quinn. How to explain that Quinn was a boyfriend-in-the-works and — Jessie believed — a little afraid of commitment? Jessie had to convince him that she was special, and being on her best behavior at that party would go far. If she could be sweet, and charming, and gracious — maybe then he'd understand how perfect they could be together.

She cleared her throat and folded her hands tightly on her lap as they pulled into the Marina. Parking was valet, no surprise there. A man in a dark suit opened her door and offered his arm. "Good evening, miss."

"Hello. Uh, good evening." She stepped out of the car and then wrapped her shawl tightly around her shoulders. Quinn was right, it was chilly.

"Thank you," he said to the valet, and handed him a few bills with the key. Then he wrapped his arm around Jessie's waist and pulled her close to his side. "You ready?"

No, she was not, but since it wasn't the time to have that debate, she put on a brave smile and said, "Ready."

Jessie was mostly unfamiliar with the trappings of wealth. Despite living for so long in a seaside town, she rarely set foot on boats. To her, this was just a yacht. A big, big yacht. As they walked up a ramp and stepped onto the deck, a gloved waiter approached and offered them flutes of champagne from a silver tray. "Madame?"

"Oh." Jessie reached for a glass, then reconsidered. Champagne had gotten her into some trouble that morning, hadn't it? "None for me, thanks."

"I'll take one." Quinn reached over to lift a flute from the tray. "Come on. There are some people I want you to meet."

Her stomach knotted. Hopefully these "people" she was meeting weren't going to want to talk about, say, laws, wealth management, or any other topics she knew exactly nothing about. Hopefully Quinn had warned them that she was just a local girl who worked at the local bakery. Maybe they'd want to talk chocolate.

On the upside, Quinn smelled nice, and his arm felt warm around her shoulders. She pulled tightly against his side and felt lucky to be with him. This could all be better than fine. This could be a lovely night.

"Hello, Quinn."

The voice was female, the tone sexy. Jessie craned her neck behind them, and her heart stopped. There stood a woman in a tight red dress. Her figure was trim and strong. Her jet-black hair was perfectly coiffed. Her face was...gah. Stunning. And the way she was looking at Quinn made Jessie want to sharpen her fingernails, had she not bitten them all to nothing.

"Hey, Caryn," Quinn said with a smile. He dropped his arm from Jessie's shoulders to turn to face her. "You look beautiful."

Caryn lifted her chin and made no effort to hide the once-over she was giving him. "You too." A quick glance at Jessie. "And is this your date?"

She swallowed a knot in her throat. Had Quinn never mentioned her name at work, or was Caryn being deliberately forgetful? Nevertheless, she held out a hand and said, "I'm Jessie."

"Hello." Her handshake was slightly limp, and the twist of her mouth suggested that Jessie was being gauche by touching her. "Quinn and I work very closely together." Emphasis on "very."

Caryn and Quinn locked eyes and seemed to share some private, unspoken joke. Either the boat was rocking, or something else was making Jessie sick to her stomach. She should've grabbed the champagne when she'd had the chance.

Still, she lifted her chin and beamed at Caryn. "Your dress is just fantastic. Red suits you."

Caryn smiled tightly and brought her flute closer to her chest. "Thanks."

"I like the beadwork." She reached out to touch, but Caryn pulled back before she made contact. "Now tell me, which store did you find this at? Because I'll have to go there next time I need something fancy to wear." She tugged at the skirt of her own dress. "I found mine on clearance."

Quinn wrapped his arm around Jessie's shoulders and pulled her back. "That's okay, Jess," he said, laughing uneasily. "No one needs to know that."

"I found this at *Belle Tique*," Caryn replied. "I don't believe they have a clearance rack, though."

Belle Tique was a high-end boutique clothing store in Spencer. Jessie, afraid she reeked of middle class, had never actually dared to set foot in there. "*Belle Tique* is a nice shop," she murmured. "I walk past sometimes and think that." Her cheeks burned.

She must have sounded pathetic, because Caryn's head tilted sympathetically at the confession. "What do you do, Jessie?"

"I work at Hedda's Bakery." Beside her, Quinn sucked in his breath, and his smile didn't quite reach his eyes. "What's wrong?" she whispered.

"You work at a bakery?" Caryn looked from her to Quinn and back to her again. "How cute. What do you do there?"

"Oh, everything, really. It's a family business, so we all chip in. I bake, wait tables, make coffee. I also have a line of chocolates that I've been developing for a while now."

Caryn and Quinn exchanged a glance and then stared at their shoes. Jessie looked down at their shoes, too. Caryn's were strappy red heels, pretty but totally impractical for that deck surface. Quinn's — well, they were just black shoes. She didn't get it.

"Anyway," she continued, "I've thought about setting off on my own and opening a chocolate shop. A chocolate *boutique*," she added.

At this, Caryn's eyes lit with interest. "How quaint. I once read a book like that. I've always thought that would be fun."

"I've encouraged Jessie to do that," Quinn said. "She needs to challenge herself more."

"But I like working with my family," Jessie said. "Plus, it's hard to find the right space. But I have it all planned out. I want a pink and white polka-dotted awning, and my shop would be called 'Chocolate Crush.'" She flared her fingers.

"Mmm. Sounds a little violent." Caryn took a sip of her champagne. "But what do I know? I'm just a lawyer."

She issued a genial laugh that had obviously been rehearsed, tossing her dark hair back slightly in the breeze. Jessie pressed her lips together and imagined herself spontaneously combusting.

"You're hardly 'just a lawyer.' Caryn has one of the firm's most high-profile cases," Quinn explained. "You may have heard about that senator who was charged with misappropriating campaign funds?"

"I work in white-collar criminal defense," she explained with a smile as her eyes flitted to Jessie and back to Quinn again. "It's a living."

"A great one," he added. "You were just named one of the top trial lawyers in the state under 40 years old. Did I congratulate you for that?"

She waved a hand. "It's nothing. You know, John Green —"

This was about the point at which Jessie's eyes lost focus and she started staring at the floorboards. Blah blah blah. Message delivered: Quinn thought Caryn was amazeballs. Jessie's cheeks hurt from forcing that smile for so long. After several more minutes passed, she'd had enough.

"Hey, did you see that ice sculpture?" She pulled at Quinn's jacket and pointed to a large, definitely bra-less ice mermaid. "She looks cold."

Quinn glanced over his shoulder before looking back at Caryn. "Yes, it's nice."

"Maybe we should walk around a little." Jessie shivered as a cool breeze brushed past her legs. Specifically, she wanted to walk into the cabin, where it

56

was certainly warmer than it was on deck, and far away from Caryn.

"Jessie's never seen the yacht before," Quinn said apologetically.

"Oh. Then you should get a tour." Caryn smiled stiffly and set a hand on Quinn's forearm. "I'm sure we'll see each other later. Nice to meet you, Jessie."

Was it her imagination, or was Caryn looking down her nose at her? "You too," she murmured.

Quinn watched Caryn walk away for a brief moment before appearing to catch himself and come back to reality. He smiled and held out his arm. "I'm guessing you want some shrimp?"

Jessie reached over and slipped her hand into the crook of his elbow, feeling her smile weaken. "Whatever. I'm not picky."

It was like Jessie had put on that dress, curled her hair, plastered her face with makeup, and promptly forgotten how much she despised these kinds of events. After a while, awash in that sea of tuxedoes, she imagined all the men as puffed-up penguins, some with fat cigars. There had been caviar and shrimp cocktail. Oysters on the half shell. Lobster tail for dinner, and a rich mousse topped with shaved chocolate and a single strawberry slice for dessert. And in between all of those courses, there had been maddening small talk and, for her, some detail fudging.

She wasn't lying, per se. More like glossing over details. What did she do for a living? She worked in the entertainment industry, which was sort of true because she *did* cater events every now and then. Where did she live? She had a little place on the beach. Again, the fact that she was currently renting an eight-hundred-square-foot cottage at a far below market rate didn't matter. Technical truth counted. But reworking the truth into something more palatable and impressive for that audience had left Jessie feeling drained by the end of the evening. She was grateful to finally have a few minutes alone with Quinn.

He was so handsome, with his strong jawline and his blond hair. He had that all-American look about him, and she thought of how she used to watch him from the bleachers as he played football when they were in high school, dreaming about the day he'd know she existed. Now there they were, on a beautiful yacht — and falling in love. Possibly. A little bit at a time. Her heart positively swelled at the thought.

As they sat in a private corner of the yacht, she rested her chin on his shoulder and said, "Want to get out of here?"

"Already?" He glanced at his watch. "We just had dessert."

"Yeah, I know, but..." She didn't complete the thought.

"But what?"

She pulled back and tightened the shawl around her shoulders. How about, *But we've barely seen each other in weeks, and you're always working, but for tonight your bosses are all drunk on a yacht and won't call you into the office?* She wanted to say that, but instead she eased back into her seat and said, "It's kind of cold."

"Here, take my jacket."

Sweet, but so not the point. "No, it's fine."

He paused, his jacket half off. "I thought you were cold?" He pulled it back on with a snap. "Sometimes I don't get you."

"Well then, that makes two of us." She smoothed her skirt down hastily. "You've put in your face time. Don't you want to go somewhere else? Like, maybe my place?"

Damn it, was it too much to ask to have sex with her own boyfriend? Did she have to come out and actually tell him what she wanted? It had been three weeks, for God's sake! Her lady parts were getting cobwebs. But Quinn patted her on the knee and said, "Later. I can't leave right now."

Jessie set her head back against the top of the seat and stared at the sky. The marina was brightly lit, and the committee of E&P wives who had planned that lovely gathering had strung white paper lanterns overhead. Scratch that — they'd *hired* someone to string the lanterns overhead. But in that little corner, the lighting was dim enough that Jessie could see the stars. "Do you ever think about what you want out of life, Quinn?"

"All the time. That's why I pull seventy-hour weeks." He leaned forward to rest his elbows on his knees. "I want partnership. Then I want to buy a place on the cliffs. A nice house overlooking the ocean, where I can have parties like this one." He looked at her. "It's expected, you know. Partners have to make the effort. All of these partners here? The entire family supports their careers."

Jessie's gaze slid to Samantha Rodriguez, who was, in her eyes, the quintessential E&P wife. Stunning. Leggy. Vivacious. She was nodding warmly as another E&P wife appeared to confide something, ever the patient ear. Samantha looked perfectly polished in a raspberry-colored dress that flattered her thin figure. *See*, she told herself, *that's how one wears color*. Jessie glanced downward at her own chartreuse attempt, and then tried to hide as much of it as possible under her shawl. "Yes, I know," she muttered. She pressed her lips together. "Is that what you want? A family?"

There was a painfully hopeful twinge to her voice as she asked. Somehow, in the hours since she'd decided to have this Conversation, she'd convinced herself that this party would give them the opportunity that several months of dating hadn't. She'd imagined that Quinn would be excited enough to see her that she would receive his undivided attention, and that just maybe, he'd be as eager as she was to talk about their future together.

Instead, he patted her knee again and said, "I think I know where this is going. Look, my entire focus has to be on partnership right now. Okay? This is the chance of a lifetime, and any setback could be disastrous." He grinned. "I'm playing the big game. I've gotta keep my head in it, lose the distractions."

She smiled feebly. "You know how I love sports metaphors." The disappointment rose in her chest. "I've had a long day, and I need to be at the bakery by five in the morning, so maybe I'll call a cab."

He issued a long sigh and stared at the deck. "You know I'm not going to let you do that." He swept his hand up and down his cheek. "I guess I've got to give you a ride."

She rose to her feet, stumbling slightly as the yacht rocked. "We can go say good-bye —"

"Nah. I'll drop you off and come back."

They headed down the walkway to the dock, back to the valet station in the marina parking lot. The drive home was quiet, the awkwardness palpable. Jessie clenched and unclenched her fists as she struggled to find the words that would make whatever was happening between them right. "Maybe we could —"

"Listen," he said, charging right into her thoughts. "I think we should take a break."

No. Her blood pooled at her feet. "Take a break?"

"Maybe not forever, but like I said, I need to put my focus on making partner. It's just not the right time for a girlfriend. You seem to want something more, and I don't want to hold you back. I'm not looking for anything serious. I thought I was clear."

They'd pulled in front of the cottage, alongside the curb. Jessie swallowed painfully, but didn't move. "You...I thought we were —"

"I don't know how to say this, so I'm just going to put it out there." He shifted in his seat to face her. "We're not a match. You're a great girl, but I guess I'm just looking for someone...different."

The breath fled her lungs as the statement settled. "You don't think I'm good enough for you," she whispered.

He covered her hand with his. "No. I didn't say that. Those are your words. But I'm busy with my career, and I need someone by my side who has certain social skills, let's say. And that's not to say that your skills aren't great, but they're *different*, you see what I'm saying?"

Jessie stared at him, slack-jawed. "No, I don't. I don't see what you're saying."

He turned away again, gripping two sides of the steering wheel and staring out into the darkness before them. "You grew up in a bakery, and that's fine. But I need someone who has a little more...business sense. Networking skills. Someone who's comfortable at these kinds of events. I mean, Jess." He looked at her. "You got drunk at a baby shower this morning."

She couldn't breathe. He may as well have slapped her. She looked down at herself, at her ugly, frumpy green dress and shawl that didn't match. So Quinn thought she wasn't good enough for him? Her skin burned with shame, and tears pricked at the corners of her eyes.

"So, are we good?" he said.

Where to start? Her brain was misfiring. "I'm thinking," she whispered.

He sighed. "Take your time. Look, I don't mean to hurt your feelings, and maybe we'll go out again some other time. Just not for now. Jess? Are you listening to me?"

She could barely focus above the pounding in her ears. Jessie wrapped her hands tightly around her clutch, pulling it closer to her chest. "I have to go."

She opened the car door and stepped outside. Without another word, she shut the door behind her and hurried to her front door. As she fit the key into the lock, she heard Quinn's car set off and drive away into the night.

Nate had turned out the lights and was climbing into bed when his cell phone rang. He reached across his nightstand, fumbling in the dark, and brought the phone to his ear. "Hello?"

"Hey buddy. I need a favor."

He cringed at the sound of the voice on the other end of the phone. Another drunk call, and these were becoming increasingly frequent. "Where are you, Quinn?"

"I dunno. Wait."

He heard him mumble incoherently and crash into something metal before coming back on the phone and saying, "You still there?"

"I'm here."

"I'm near Landry's. By the steps."

Landry's was a bar on the other side of town. "You stay there. Sit on the steps, okay?" Nate flung off the sheets and set his bare feet on the floorboards. "Quinn? Did you hear me?"

In response, Nate heard a choke in Quinn's voice, followed by a muffled sob. His heart clenched. "What happened?" He didn't wait for a response before grabbing his keys and reaching for his jeans. Had Quinn tried to drive in this condition? It wouldn't have been the first time. "Talk to me. Are you in trouble?" He was already pulling on his pants.

"No." Quinn sniffed. "Yes."

It sounded more like "yesh." He must've been drinking for hours. "I'm on my way. Do you need me to call for help? Tell me what happened."

The question sent Quinn slurring into the receiver, his voice cracking. "I was with her, man."

Nate froze, one leg of his pants dangling loosely. "You were with who?" He regretted the question the second he heard it out loud. He didn't want to hear the answer.

"Caryn." Quinn's voice was suddenly quiet, as if the admission had sobered him. "I hooked up with Caryn."

Nate's blood went cold. "Shit, man." He looked out the bedroom window at the moon, hanging heavy and white in the sky. "Caryn?"

He heard the sound of a siren passing close to Quinn. When the sound passed, Quinn said, "I think I love her."

Damn it. Nate zipped and buttoned his jeans and reached for a sweatshirt. "Sit tight. I'm on my way." He pulled on a pair of running shoes and headed out the door.

This was the way it had been for as long as Nate could remember. He and Quinn had been inseparable from the first day of kindergarten because they complimented each other so well. Quinn was the bold one, the team sport jock. Captain of the football and lacrosse teams, top of his class academically. Serious and smart, but with an irresponsible streak. He had a tendency to get himself into the hot seat on a regular basis, but he had a knack for talking his way out of most problems. For all the other ones, Nate was there.

He thought of their many misadventures as he made the drive to Landry's. Where had it started? Probably with sneaking cookies from the jar at home. Then there were the pranks at school, like that time Quinn bought twenty rolls of crepe paper in school colors and decorated the trees for homecoming, or that time he organized a secret after-hours party in the high school pool. Kid stuff, really, and Nate had loved being a part of it. But then Nate grew up. If he'd ever enjoyed partying — and he wasn't sure he had — he didn't any more. He had a business to run and a life to manage. He didn't have the energy to spend nights at the bar the way Quinn did. Or to lie about it.

That was the part that killed him, that Quinn was out most nights at a bar, not working late like he told Jessie. To her, he was some sainted hard worker, toiling into the wee hours at his desk. More like _her_, because she'd been pulling double shifts for years now. It was like Quinn knew exactly what to say to Jessie to keep her hanging on no matter how awful he was to her. _Hey, babe. You know I'm working for partnership._ And Jessie would relay the conversation to Nate. "Oh, well," she'd say with a sunny smile and a shrug of her shoulders. "He's trying to make something of himself. I understand completely."

Sometimes Nate wondered whether his loyalty had become misplaced somewhere along the course of their friendship.

As he drew closer to the bar, Nate resolved to tell his friend the truth. "You're thirty years old, man. Time to grow up. Stop hanging out in bars every night." When what he wanted to say was, "Do whatever you want, but leave Jessie out of it. Just leave her alone." She was a sweet girl, and she deserved the truth. But he knew as he pulled up into an alley beside Landry's that he would say what he always did, which was nothing at all.

Quinn looked like hell, but at least he hadn't been sick...yet. When he climbed into the passenger seat, Nate handed him a gym towel from the backseat and said, "Keep this in your lap."

His friend's head bobbed around like he understood, but he didn't reply other than to say, "Thanks." Like handing him a towel was some massive gesture of goodwill.

Nate clenched his jaw as he backed out of the driveway next to Landry's, avoiding a drunken group of college kids who weren't dressed for the chilly evening. Listen to him — when did he become an old man?

Beside him, Quinn mumbled, "Girls're hot," and craned his neck to get a better look.

"Jesus, Quinn. Get a grip!" Nate shook his head, speeding away from the ugly scene once he hit the road. "What the hell happened to you tonight?"

Quinn squeezed his eyes shut, wincing as if the very question hurt him. "I slept with Caryn."

"I got that part."

Quinn leaned his head back against the seat and turned to Nate. His eyes roamed as he struggled to focus. "She wanted to go out. I said okay."

Nate's knuckles whitened. He didn't understand what Quinn saw in Caryn. Sure, she was pretty — beautiful, even — but their very brief, very volatile relationship seemed to consist of fight after argument after threats to never speak to each other again. Caryn had dumped Quinn for someone else after a few months of combustion, and Quinn hadn't eaten for days. When he'd invited Quinn out to Sam's, Nate had just been trying to cheer up his friend. That had been a mistake. Jessie had been there that night. Next thing he knew, Jessie Mallory, the girl Nate had been renting a cottage to and working up the nerve to ask out, was Quinn's rebound. Worse, she liked him. A lot.

"So you went out." The words barely squeezed through Nate's lips. "Where'd you go?"

"Her place." When Nate groaned, Quinn hastened to add, "She's going through a tough time. She needed to talk. I don't know where we stand right now. I mean, it was like old times, but better. Then we were done, and suddenly she's telling me to leave." He gazed down at his hands as they lay open and limp in his lap. "I don't get women."

"So you walked from Caryn's house to Landry's?"

"Pretty much." He fisted the towel and turned it to get a better look under the light cast by the streetlamps. "This is a nice towel."

Nate wasn't willing to change the subject so easily. "You've been sitting in Landry's drinking alone all night? You should've called me."

Quinn made an attempt to shrug, but it came off sloppy. "You wouldn't get it. Me and Caryn...we have a thing. Only we understand."

"What about Jessie?"

"What about her?" Quinn asked, sounding as if she wasn't even part of the equation. Sounding, Nate realized with a chill, almost as if he'd forgotten about her.

He gritted his teeth as he rounded the corner to Quinn's house. They were only a few blocks from Landry's, but his friend couldn't have made the walk. His head lolled around as if he was struggling to keep it upright.

Nate told himself not to lose it. No lectures. He was being Quinn's friend now, not Jessie's. But damn it if he didn't want to grab Quinn by the shoulders and demand to know what was wrong with him. "Jessie's a great girl," he said, measuring each word. "She doesn't deserve to be cheated on."

His friend was silent for a stretch before reaching up to rub his cheek with the palm of his hand and saying, "Me and Jessie are over."

Nate froze. "You two broke up?"

"Yeah. We weren't ever serious. I just...it was just for fun. She's not my type."

Nate mulled this over in his mind as he brought the vehicle to a stop in the driveway. So Jessie was single again? That wasn't the worst thing he'd heard all day. "Do you need help getting out?"

"Nah, I got it. Just a little buzzed." Even as he said it, he frowned at the seat belt buckle and made three jabs at the button before managing to get loose. "I'll be all right in a couple hours. Thanks again, buddy." He clapped Nate on the shoulder.

"Good night."

Nate waited until Quinn got into his house safely. It took him a couple of tries to unlock his door, but then he raised one hand and gave a sheepish smile. Nate shook his head and backed slowly out of the driveway, thinking of Jessie. Somehow, he imagined she'd be handling the breakup differently than Quinn.

He took a detour to drive past her cottage, though he didn't know why. It wasn't like he was going to wander up to the door and tell her he was in the neighborhood. His heart sank when he saw that her lights were still on. Not good. Was there any reason he could stop in, just say he was checking on her? He glanced at the clock. No, not at this hour. Nothing about that would be normal. Besides, he had a client appointment first thing in the morning, and he should get home, too.

He swallowed and continued down the street. He hoped she was all right, and that she'd just fallen asleep on the couch again. Quinn and Caryn? Bad news. But Jessie being single again? Nate felt a surge of hope.

Maybe.

CHAPTER FOUR

THE BOTTOM STAIR in the back was groaning again. Nate winced. He'd just fixed the darn thing, right before giving the staircase a fresh coat of white paint. He'd have to take a look at it when he came home to make sure it was an annoyance, and nothing structural. He had a tenant on the first floor, and he couldn't take the chance that anyone got hurt. The joys of owning rental property.

The cool breeze rolling in from the ocean dulled the headache that came from too little sleep the night before. He zipped his jacket and hesitated before climbing into his SUV. From this spot, he could see the sun rising over the water, turning it pink and orange. These were things in life worth pausing for, but he was only looking for a convenient excuse to stop. He was on his way to see Claire Burgess, and, well...He needed to give his coffee a few more minutes to work its magic.

He liked Claire, just as he liked most people. He'd been training her for almost a year now, and they'd developed a rapport. Despite Jessie's jokes — all of which were fair, he had to admit — Claire took her fitness seriously, and she was committed to being healthier. That's all he could ask as a personal trainer. As a *man*, though...Claire was a challenge.

The ride to Great Barrington at that time of day took less than twenty minutes. Nate drove along the coast to enjoy the view of the sunrise and the waves breaking against the rocks. When he pulled up to Claire's house, he only had to wait a moment for security to open the gates. Then he continued down the crushed rock drive, watching the mansion rise into view: gray stone, large windows, and shrubs pruned into decorative patterns. Four chimneys and a fountain out front. All of it purchased with old money that Claire's great-grandfather had acquired selling liquor during Prohibition. Sometimes crime paid very well.

He pulled into the usual spot, closer to the doorway so as not to block the gardeners' trucks. That morning, Claire was waiting for him on the front steps, clutching a steaming cup of something. Herbal tea if he had to guess, since she didn't go for coffee.

"Morning, sweetness," she said, and tilted her neck to the side in a stretch. "You're just in time for tea."

"Thanks, I'm all set. I had a cup of coffee before I left."

"Mmm." She wrinkled her nose. "I never could touch the stuff."

See, now this was where she got to be a challenge, because as she said that, she grazed a hand slowly down her side and rested it on her waist. Then she blew the steam over the top of her mug with stained lips, eyeing him the entire time. Nate pulled a box of rubber resistance straps from the back of his car and tried to ignore the flirtation. That and the tight raspberry-pink top she was wearing that left nothing to the imagination. "Today we're working on flexibility."

"Oh, that's my absolute favorite. I love the way you stretch me out, Nate." Said mildly, with another arch of the neck. "You have the best positions."

He took a deep breath. It was going to be a long morning. Now, if Jessie ever talked to him like that, he'd probably lose his head completely. There was a thought.

"We're going to do a warm-up first, right?" Claire took a sip of her tea and then nodded to the massive wooden door behind her. "Let's go this way. We can run on the beach."

"The weather's finally nice enough."

"You're telling me, sweetness. The winter's been so terrible that if it gets above seventy degrees today, I'm sunbathing topless. I don't even care."

Despite its size, Claire's home was warm. It looked like something out of those catalogues his tenant was always getting, the ones Jessie made him look through with her. Lots of sheer curtains and tile, area rugs and couches with different-colored throw pillows. It was nice, he had to admit. The furnishings, and the floor-to-ceiling windows that faced the Atlantic. He could look at that all day, watch the sailboats glide across the water in the warmer weather.

Claire set her mug down on the black counter in the kitchen. Soapstone, but he only knew that because he'd remodeled the kitchen in the cottage before Jessie moved in. The old cabinets were flimsy, and he'd thought it was time for an upgrade. They'd gone shopping together and made a few weekends out of selecting white maple cabinets and picking a slab of gray granite. The end result had been better than he could've done alone. If it had been up to him, he would've walked into a store and pointed to the first cabinet and counter style he'd seen. He wasn't a shopper, but with Jessie, well. Things were more fun.

His pulse kicked. She was a great girl. And now she was single, which meant he could finally tell her how he felt. The thought sent sparks through his stomach. He'd never been good at that kind of thing. Not like Quinn, whose confidence had been stoked by the attention of all the girls in school. No one in Archer Cove High School paid attention to a track star, no matter how many records he smashed. When the challenge involved something physical, he could achieve. But when the challenge was emotional, he became tongue-tied.

"We'll go through the solarium," Claire explained as she slid open a glass door. A rush of heat greeted them. "It gets so stuffy in here. But the plants love it, and it's nice to sit in here in the winter."

They exited into an English-style garden with multiple levels and followed a series of slate stairs down to the grass. Once there, they took a steep wooden staircase to the beach. "All right. We'll do a fifteen-minute run," Nate said. "You ready to start?"

She ran a hand through her chin-length red hair. "Let's do it."

They set off down the beach, close to the waves, where the sand was firm. There was nothing quite like running on the beach, and within a few minutes, his legs started to burn pleasantly. "You know, you've come a long way, Claire. You remember the first time we did this?"

"I thought I was going to pass out," she laughed. "Now I actually head out here alone sometimes. I have fewer back problems, too."

"That's good to hear." His focus with his clients was always on functional fitness: not building huge muscles necessarily, but making their bodies better at performing daily living tasks.

"I'm probably going to make you blush," she said, and eyed him sidelong. "Look at that. I didn't even say it yet!"

"Am I blushing?" Probably. He could only imagine what was about to come out of her mouth.

"Yes, you are. But I was going to say that you've made a difference in my life. Have you ever thought about opening your own place? Because if you ever decided to go that route, I'd invest in your business."

Nate focused on his breath and the pounding of his heart as he digested her words. "You'd invest in a gym?"

"Is that what you'd do, open up a gym?" She bobbed her head. "I think it would be fantastic, knowing what I

74

know about you. Then clients could visit, and you wouldn't spend all of your time driving around to meet them. Look at you! Your face is all red."

"I'm trying to keep up with you," he joked, but she was right, his face was burning. He struggled to process the compliment and the possibilities. "That means a lot. Thank you."

Not that he could ever take her money. He had some saved up, and he figured if the time was ever right, he could apply for a loan.

"I'm offering you money here, sweetheart. Money from the sky! Low-interest loan. We'll work something out. You say the word and I'll have my attorney draw up some papers. I'm looking to diversify my investments, and I'd like to put something back into the community. Local businesses, you see what I mean?" She waved a hand. "I'm getting winded. You think about it. Promise me."

Nate's heart was pounding harder than it should have been, but he nodded. "Yeah. Okay. I promise."

He doubted he could ever take Claire's money. If he was going to open a gym, he alone had to take responsibility for its success or failure.

She turned her head to stare and made a show of looking him up and down. "You still single? Look at those leg muscles. Someone needs to snatch you up."

He groaned and shook his head. "All right. Let's turn around and head back at that rock up ahead."

Jessie woke ahead of the alarm. Or maybe she hadn't slept at all. She couldn't be sure. All she knew was that when she slumped to the bathroom and peered into the mirror, her eyes were puffy and red from crying. When she thought about the last words that Quinn had said to her, the shame burned in her chest.

Different social skills. What did that mean? She thought of all of the beautiful E&P wives and how elegant they were. Was she some sort of clumsy Neanderthal to him? She showered quickly and pulled her long hair back into a braid. By the time she was dressed, Jessie decided she was in a very foul mood.

She poured a bowl of cereal and milk and stood at the counter, watching Prince Travis. He looked like he was scowling. "I understand, Travis," she said. "Bad moods are contagious, though, so you may want to turn that frown upside down."

Well, so she was sounding like her father, who had the gene that predisposed people to be perpetually optimistic salesmen. Had he been born twenty years earlier, he would have gone door-to-door selling vacuums, she had no doubt. His particular talents had landed him in computer sales and taken him literally around the world. But whatever gene Dad had, Jessie lacked completely. Or so she would have thought, and yet here she was, pitching Dad-isms to her stuffed fox. "Never mind, Travis. You can be pissed off if you want to. Go ahead and let it eat you up on the inside."

Her ego was bruised, no denying it. To Quinn, she was some nobody who worked in a bakery and played with chocolate recipes in her spare time. She didn't know why she kept turning that thought over, because it sure stung, and she was hurting enough as it was.

She went through the workday mechanically and didn't mention anything to Uncle Hank or Emily. She was grateful that the bakery was busy. The normalcy of the routine helped. Then, as she left work for the night, she hit a wall of feelings.

Humiliation at not being good enough.

The shame that she had been judged based on growing up in a bakery.

Anger at the injustice.

Fear that she was unlovable.

She needed to snap herself out of it. There were things to look forward to, and plenty of distractions. That's when she remembered the dress that Wren had given her. She'd forgotten to try it on.

Jessie walked into her bedroom and opened the closet. She'd hung the dress in the center, and she slipped her fingers greedily across the fabric, feeling them glide. Now that she turned the fabric, she saw that it wasn't true sapphire, but that the color was translucent, shifting and changing with the direction of the light. She held it up to admire the plunge of the neckline and the elegant drape of the material. It was simple, but exquisite. "Beautiful," she breathed.

Jessie quickly disrobed. The dress fell easily down her body. *Custom-made*, she thought as she admired it in the full-length mirror. She'd never worn anything like it before. She began to zip up the back. Then the zipper resisted. She froze.

The dress was too tight.

"No," she whispered, and tried again. Sure enough, the zipper wouldn't budge.

She held her breath and sucked in her gut. She tried pressing the layer of fat on her back down and sliding the zipper over it. Nothing. Nada. Her gorgeous, custom-made dress didn't fit. "Damn it."

Jessie considered her shape in the mirror. Custom-made. The dressmaker had taken her measurements, what? Three months ago? And since then, she'd enlarged to the point she no longer fit in the dress. It was enough to make her want to stuff a truffle in her face.

Which may have been the reason she was in that mess to begin with.

She carefully peeled the dress off her form and told herself not to cry. This was not something to cry over. She could return it for a larger size. But then, oh right — it had been custom-made to fit her perfectly. Just...damn it.

She pulled on the pair of gray sweatpants she'd been favoring lately, realizing with a sinking feeling that she'd been wearing them because they were so roomy and forgiving. Then she ran to the bathroom. Her scale was lodged behind the toilet, the space issue being what it was. She could practically sit on the toilet and shower at the same time, and it wasn't like she needed to weigh herself daily. Though perhaps more often...

She stepped onto the scale and frowned at the number. No, the dial must be off. She stepped down again and checked. The dial wasn't off. *By the pastry-loving lips of Saint Elizabeth.* She'd gained fifteen pounds.

All right. No problem. This was not a problem. Still, Jessie bit her lower lip to keep from crying as she walked back into the kitchen and retrieved the magnetic calendar from her refrigerator. Desperate times called for plans, that was all. She traced the dry-erase marker across the weeks. It was mid-May and the wedding wasn't until the middle of August, so if she lost three pounds a week on average, then she would be fitting into that dress by July. Perfect.

Jessie set the calendar back on the refrigerator, but it didn't take long for the sense of victory to wear off. Three pounds a week. Her job was to create chocolates. She experimented with recipes. She basically made a living eating chocolate. Though perhaps she could take smaller bites.

Her heart was heavy as she slumped into the chair before the fireplace. Then it hit her. This could be the change she was looking for: she could slim down, but why stop there? If Jessie wanted to actually feel good about her life, then major changes were in order.

She grabbed a pen and a pad of paper and went to work, furiously detailing all of her faults. She was a little flighty, that was for sure. She still blushed as she remembered her speech at the baby shower on Sunday. How could she expect herself to be the kind of person

Quinn would love if she acted so irresponsibly? *Must think more before speaking. Or acting.*

And what else? She tapped her pen against her lips. She worked hard at the bakery, and enjoyed what she did, and frankly she didn't see the need to strike out on her own. Perhaps, though, this was unambitious of her? Jessie frowned at the paper as she wrote, *Be more ambitious.* The thought of leaving Hedda's sent her pulse racing. Being out on her own, without Uncle Hank? What would she do without him?

She swallowed and set down her hand again to write, *Be fearless.* Underlined it twice.

By the end of the evening, Jessie had carefully considered all of her flaws. Fortunately, she had also decided how to fix them. Satisfied, she pulled a blanket over herself and settled back against the couch, where she soon fell asleep.

The text from Jessie read, "Emergency. Pizza. Meme's." Like he was some kind of mind reader.

Except Nate knew exactly what she'd meant, and he'd dropped everything, gotten in his car, and driven to the spot.

Meme's Pizza was located in an old chapel in the center of the downtown, and the owners had kept a lot of the original touches and architecture when they'd converted the space to a pizza restaurant. The windows were still stained glass, and a large brick oven sat in the spot where the altar used to be. The pizza itself was great, but the building's history was a large part of the draw. Since Jessie had started dating Quinn, the three of them had met there a few times.

A piece of him was relieved she'd reached out first, because for the past two days, he'd been trying to come up with a plan to contact Jessie, just to check in on her, without being too obvious about it. He didn't want her to know that he knew about the breakup. He didn't want her to think they'd been talking about her. Much better that she should tell him herself.

Jessie was already seated at Meme's Pizza when he arrived. She was sitting at a small round table covered in a white-and-red checked tablecloth, frowning with impressive concentration at a large laminated menu. Her blonde hair was down for a change, and she wore it in loose curls. She looked so pretty it hurt.

He'd dressed up more than usual. Not that this was a date. Just two friends meeting for Tuesday-night pizza. They'd order a pitcher of beer and complain, and they'd leave feeling better, aside from the indigestion. But he'd changed into khakis and a light sweater, and he'd even put on some cologne. He stepped forward then, and she looked up when he was a few strides from the table. Jessie smiled brightly and said, "You look nice."

His pulse kicked a few beats in response, but he pulled out his chair, the picture of calm. "You do, too."

She picked up the end of a curl and flicked it behind her shoulder. "Thanks. Want to split an IPA? I'm feeling bitter."

Uh oh. "Sure. Sounds good." He took a seat just as a waiter came over with a pitcher of beer and two pint glasses.

"Great, because that's what I ordered." She poured a glass for each of them and raised hers. "Cheers."

"What are we drinking to tonight?"

"Shoot, I don't know. How about if we drink to the adoption of orphaned kittens?"

"To kittens." He raised his glass.

She took a generous gulp and set the glass down with a sigh. "So, I'm thinking about making a change. A big one."

Nate was half-listening, half-scanning the appetizers. "You're going to drop this on me now? We haven't even ordered."

She pulled the menu from his hands and set it to the side, on top of her own. "You already know what you're getting. You get the same thing every time. We're going to split a large pizza, half Hawaiian and half sausage and peppers. You'll say that my half is disgusting and that pineapple doesn't belong on pizza, but you'll eat it anyway after you've finished your half." She wrapped her fingers around the bottom of her glass and pouted her lower lip. "It's always the same. Every day. Everything here. It never changes."

Nate sat back in his chair, feeling like he was under attack. "Is there somewhere else you want to be?"

"No. Don't take it personally." She unfolded her napkin and a metal knife and fork clattered against the table. "I'm just saying...you know how it is. You grew up here too. Everyone knows everyone else. Their business. It's always the same."

Something about that statement scratched at him. "You love the Archer Cove community."

Damn, he didn't mean to sound so injured. But wasn't he one of those things that was always around, cluttering up her day with the familiar? He took a breath. "So where's Quinn? I take it he couldn't make it?"

She picked up her beer, but then her face crumpled and she just sat there, holding her drink in midair and crying. Good lord.

"I'm sorry." Nate kicked himself. What a jackass he was! He wrested the pint glass from her fist and set it carefully down on the table. "We'll talk about something else."

"He..." Her face turned red, and the tears streamed freely. "We're taking a break."

"No, we don't have to talk about it. Let's talk about how boring everything is here." Out of the frying pan and into the fire. Damn it!

Nate had heard some women talk about "ugly crying," which he guessed was what women got self-conscious about these days, looking too emotional or something. Not Jessie. She sat there in the middle of the restaurant and bawled her eyes out. Nate stared at his hands, unsure where he should be directing his gaze. Not at her face. He wasn't supposed to look at how splotchy her cheeks were getting, because that was rude...right? Damn, he didn't know enough about women and all of their unspoken rules.

He swallowed and then handed her a napkin, avoiding eye contact. "Do you...want to use mine?" he muttered.

She accepted the napkin, but just gripped it in one hand and used the other to swipe at her cheeks. "What did I do, Nate?"

"Nothing." Now he thought he could safely look at her. He leaned over and set his hand over hers. "Listen to me: Jess, you didn't do *anything*."

Quinn was his best friend. Had been his best friend since the first day of kindergarten, and nothing had ever come between them. Not school, or sports, or girls. But seeing Jessie cry like this made him want to pummel him right then.

She pulled closer and set her face against his shoulder. Her hair smelled like soap and flowers. It tickled his cheek. He wrapped his arms around her and held her while she cried, smoothing his hand down her back. She was so soft. "I'm sorry," he whispered. His chest hurt.

A waiter who looked to be fresh out of high school came over then and gave them a shy smile, pencil and pad in hand. "Are you ready to order?"

"No," Nate said. Was this kid serious?

Jessie pulled back then and covered her face with her napkin. "Just give us a minute, please?"

The waiter stuck the pencil behind his ear and stuffed the pad into his apron. When he was out of earshot, Nate mumbled, "You want to get something to go instead?"

"No. I don't want to be alone."

Jeez, was he invisible or something? Not worth arguing about. Call it guilt over his friend's insensitivity, but he'd close down the restaurant with her if that was what she wanted. "Suits me fine," he said. "I don't have any client appointments tomorrow morning, anyway."

The tears were over, at least. She sniffed and eyed the menu. "I feel like eating popcorn shrimp. You should stop me."

"No ma'am. I'm not making that mistake again. You get what you want."

She blew some hair off her face and pouted at the menu, looking defeated. "I should eat a salad."

"Jess." He pulled the menu out of her hands. "Talk to me."

She set the menu aside with exaggerated patience and folded her hands on the table, but she refused to meet his eyes, instead setting her gaze somewhere off toward the restrooms. "Jess?" he tried again. This time he watched her return to him, slow as molasses, but eventually getting to where he needed her to be. "What's going on?"

She didn't cry. She pulled her hands into her lap and said, "I knew that things weren't going well. I've known for a long time. And then last night was just horrible." She shuddered.

Nate recoiled as he thought of how badly things had actually gone, and how unlikely it was that Jessie knew the first thing about it, but he recovered quickly. He was supposed to be offering support, not making it worse. "So the party was...stuffy?"

Her eyes widened as if to ask him how clueless he was. Then she said, "No, the party was amazing. Everything was so perfect and...luxurious, and the E&P

85

wives are all gorgeous, of course. Then I was wearing this chartreuse dress. That's green, by the way," she added. "I don't know. It wasn't super high quality, but I wouldn't say it was cheap, either, but I felt cheap in it. I felt like I didn't belong at all, like maybe they were all laughing at me."

The statement struck him somewhere square in the chest. He winced. "That's a terrible way to feel."

"Yes. It is." She took a sip of her beer and sat back in her seat, appearing to mull over the statement." And then Quinn told me that he needed someone different by his side. Someone who had a more sophisticated business sense and not — how did he put it? Bakery social skills."

Nate blinked. "Wait. Is that what he said? Those words came out of his mouth?"

"Close." She said it calmly, almost as if she were resigned. "I've spent so much of my life being the outsider. In high school, I was the kid whose parents had moved to Europe and left her to live with her uncle and cousin in a cramped apartment. Now I look around and see that everyone else is advancing in interesting careers, getting married, and having babies. I kind of want to be like everyone else for a change." She looked at him. "Do you think that's wrong?"

The way she was watching him right then, like she was looking for something, anything, to hold onto, well. It tore him up inside. "Hell no, it's not wrong," he said quietly. "There's nothing wrong with what you've said. It's just that..." He paused, not knowing what should follow.

"I think you're great the way you are, and if Quinn can't see that, it's his problem. That's all."

She smiled sadly and tipped her glass to tap against his. "Cheers. Thanks for that."

He eyed her over the rim of his glass. "What else? There's something you're not telling me."

She pulled her chair closer to his — so close that their legs touched, and a thrill shot up his side. Jessie didn't seem to notice as she pulled a slip of paper out of her handbag. "I've made a list of my faults. I'm going to fix them. All of them."

He blinked twice at her. "Wait. You did — you wrote —"

"I made a list of my faults," she said, more slowly. "And I'm going to fix them. Quinn will make partner in August, and then he'll be ready for a relationship again. By that time, I will be a whole new person." She smiled. "The woman of his dreams. And I want you to help me."

*Oh for the love of...*Nate shifted back in his seat and reached for his beer. "Jess. Come on." He paused, curiosity getting the best of him. "Let me see the list."

She brought the folded piece of paper closer to her chest. "I'm not ready to share it."

"You want me to mold you into the perfect woman, is that it? But you won't even show me what's on that piece of paper?"

Her lips thinned as she considered the question, and moment by moment, she relaxed her shoulders and brought the paper away from her chest." I guess when you put it that way...but you can't laugh. You have to promise me."

"You're coming to me, looking for my professional advice. I will be the paragon of professionalism."

He sort of meant it, but she didn't look convinced. Reluctantly, she handed over the paper. *Jackpot.*

Nate could barely contain his interest as he unfolded the paper. Was this —? Yes, it was. Pink stationery. With purple flowers at the top. She was so darn cute that Nate started to smile despite himself. Then he saw what she'd written, and the smile dropped away.

1. Problem: bakery social skills.
Solution: Must think before speaking. Or acting.**
2. Problem: headed nowhere professionally.
Solution: Must be more ambitious. Must be fearless. Open chocolate shop to demonstrate both.
3. Problem: headed nowhere personally —> perhaps due to bakery social skills (BSS)?
Solution: Must comply with #1 and #2. Small talk is critical.
4. Problem: don't fit dress.
Solution: Lose three pounds a week times five weeks.

**N.B. No more mimosas. They are marketed as classy, but are actually the devil. Also, because of empty calories and sugars.

It was like a dark cloud blackening his mood. Was this what Jessie thought of herself? "Bakery social skills?" he murmured. What the hell did that mean?

She took that as an invitation to remove the paper from his hands in one quick gesture and refold it into a small square. "I don't think it's my fault, per se. I haven't been exposed to more cultured matters, that's all. I also haven't challenged myself as much as I should have. I'm optimistic that all of this can be fixed." Jessie tucked the paper back into her bag and settled back in her seat, turning her wide, hopeful eyes to him. "Well? Do you think you can help me?"

Man, did he want to be invisible right then. He'd haul ass right out of that restaurant and pretend he'd never even seen that list. Nate couldn't explain the sudden raw, sick feeling in his gut, like he'd seen something he shouldn't have. "I don't think I'm your guy." He didn't want to change her. As far as he was concerned, she was great the way she was.

Her face fell, and for a minute he thought she was going to cry again. "Oh. That's okay," she said.

"It's just that I don't — what do I know about social skills? I wasn't born into that kind of a lifestyle."

"But Quinn's your best friend. I thought you'd have some insight into how I could develop country club manners." She bit her lower lip. "Forget it. Just please don't say anything about that list. To Quinn, or anyone. I can't stand the thought of people laughing at me."

She swallowed and inched closer to the table, keeping her gaze on the plate in front of her. "I would never laugh at you," Nate said. Not to be cruel. Not when she'd shown him how vulnerable she was.

They spent the rest of the meal avoiding the subject altogether, and Nate hoped that was a good sign. Then, as they were leaving, she whispered, "I still love him. I just want to do everything I can to show him who I am." She turned to Nate with wide eyes. "Does that make sense?"

The words wrapped around his heart and squeezed. For a moment, his throat closed and the words wouldn't come. Hell yeah, it made sense. Because all he wanted was to show Jessie who *he* was.

He looked down at his feet, and at the stretch of asphalt between them, and he thought about her list. If he was honest, he could write one of his own. On it, he'd want to be a better friend to Jessie, a better man who could show her what she was worth. Hell, he could stand to be fearless and to take risks, too. Open his own place and make a go of it. Maybe he should throw "be less judgmental" on there, because what was wrong with wanting to show someone your best side, anyway?

"It makes sense," he said, and took a deep breath. "Look, I'll help you if I can, all right? If you want me to put together a training program for you, or a nutrition plan, I can do that." Maybe she'd make a few changes and feel better about herself. No harm there.

Her blue eyes widened, and a cautious smile spread across her lips. "Thank you. That would be great."

In the parking lot, she gave him a one-armed hug — their usual good-bye. Noncommittal. Then they took their separate cars home. He'd meant it when he'd said that he thought Jessie was great the way she was. If he could change one thing about her, it would be that she'd stop chasing after things she'd never be able to catch and start seeing what was in front of her.

CHAPTER FIVE

WHEN NATE CHECKED his cell phone the next morning, there was a message from George Dinardo. His stomach sparked and his pulse kicked. "Nate. George Dinardo, returning your call. Look, I'm gonna be around this morning doing some work on the space. If you want to stop by we can talk then. I should be there early. Say by eight. If not, we'll set up another time."

Nate glanced at the clock. Eight o'clock, huh? That gave him a full three hours to get ready. Perfect.

He had a light schedule that day. He was doing some physical therapy work later in the afternoon, and before that he was offering yoga at the country club. That ought to be interesting. His buddy was running a rec program there and had asked him for a favor. He wouldn't say he was the best yoga instructor in the world, but his friend was desperate, and Nate figured he could get by well enough.

He parked his SUV in a street space by the food shelf and saw the director, Tom Hannigan, lifting a cardboard box from the trunk of his red Buick. "Hey, Tom. Let me help you with that." Nate hurried to his side.

Tom had suffered a mild stroke a few years ago, and as he unloaded the box into Nate's arms, he said, "Thank you. It's not too heavy, but it saves me a trip." He reached into the trunk and lifted a white plastic bag weighted with canned goods before closing the door. "Donations have been low."

"And I'm guessing need has been high." Nate glanced into the box he was carrying. There were a few boxes of pasta, a jar of sauce, and assorted canned foods. Condensed milk, peas, and creamed corn.

"It seems to be the way it goes." Tom sighed. "But some folks are finally getting back on their feet. It's been a long stretch."

The food shelf was a squat, square building that had once housed a laundromat. Yellow curtains hung on tension rods halfway down the front windows, giving privacy to those inside. Tom unlocked the front door and turned on the lights. The interior was an open room lined with shelves, much like a grocery store. Tom always stressed the need for people to come in and take what they needed with a sense of dignity, like they were shopping in the general store. The shelves appeared well-stocked with loaves of bread, boxes of pasta and noodles, assorted vegetables, nut butters and jellies. It was enough to keep some families going when they needed help the most.

Tom stood just under six feet tall, but he was broad-shouldered and round in the middle. His thick hair was silver on top and dark gray at the temples, and his face was kind. If he'd grown a beard, he probably could've played Santa at the town Christmas festival — appropriate, considering he spent his life giving to others.

Nate set the box down on a folding table in front and removed some of the canned goods. "I'll help you unload."

"Sandra should be here any minute," Tom said with a glance at the clock on the wall. It was shaped like a smiling cat, and a swinging black tail kept the seconds. "She's buying some perishables."

"I don't have anywhere else to be right now," Nate said easily, and checked the date on the cans before setting them on the shelf.

"I'm actually glad you're here," Tom said. "I could use some expert advice."

Nate chuckled. "You've mistaken me for someone else, sir. Though I'm faking my way through yoga this afternoon. I like to pretend to help people."

"You're too modest." Tom set his hands on his waist and stood for a moment, catching his breath. "We need a new roof. We're eligible for a grant, but it will only cover half the cost of repairs. We have to run a fundraiser."

"Uh huh." Nate continued to straighten the cans on the shelf, his body half-turned toward Tom. "And let me guess: you're auctioning off bachelors?"

"We were thinking more along the lines of a road race."

Nate paused, one hand on a can of string beans. "What distance?"

Tom shrugged. "You tell me. We'd like to get as many participants as possible. What's the best distance for that?"

"I'd say five kilometers. It's a friendly distance for organizers and runners. You won't need the resources that a longer race would require."

"Good, 'cause we're stretched pretty thin there." Tom slipped his hands into his pockets. "We were hoping to plan it for the end of June, but we don't know where to start."

"End of —?" Nate straightened and turned to face the director. "Tom. It's mid-May. Do you have a course? Permits? Have you done advertising of any kind?"

He lifted his shoulders. "No to all. We're in a bind. We thought we'd get another year out of the roof, but with all of the ice last winter...well, we just found out we need to replace it this summer. Fall at the latest."

"Which is why you need to host a race in June." Nate dragged his palm down his face. "These things can take months to plan."

"We only have weeks," Tom replied. "I was just hoping you'd point us in the right direction. You've planned a few of these things, haven't you? I don't want to take up a lot of your time. If you can share some tips, great. If not..."

The director turned with a shrug and headed toward the front of the room. Nate swept a hand across the back of his neck. He'd first volunteered at the food shelf when he was sixteen years old, and he'd always liked Tom — quiet, unassuming Tom, who never asked for anything. A 5K? Nate couldn't think of anything that Tom was likely to know less about. Between his inexperience and the timing, it was a disaster waiting to happen.

Nate stared at the shelves. Archer Cove was a town where disparity was the norm. It was populated with people who had more than enough and those who struggled to make ends meet. Lots of families needed to be able to count on something like the food shelf. And the food shelf needed a new roof.

He released a long breath. So planning a race on such short notice was a challenge. Nate was an athlete — since when did he back down from a challenge?

"Tom, stop," Nate said. "I'll do it."

Tom paused and glanced over his shoulder. "You'll give me some tips? That's great. I'd really app —"

"No. I mean I'll plan the event for you. I've planned a bunch of races in the area over the years. I'll dust off some old routes."

Tom seemed momentarily stunned. As he came out of it, he shook his head slowly. "You're one of a kind, Nate. I mean that."

"It's no trouble. Off the top of my head, I have a few ideas already."

As Nate told him his thoughts, Tom's eyes softened and his broad shoulders relaxed as if a weight were being lifted. Finally he said, "I can't tell you how much I appreciate this. Some of our board members suggested that we sponsor a race to raise some extra money. I don't know the first thing about it." He patted his stomach and laughed. "As you can see, I'm not much of a runner. If there's anything I can do —"

"If this is going to be successful, we need to involve local businesses. I'll make a few calls, but we should get sponsors lined up as quickly as possible." Weeks ago, really.

"I'll call people today." Tom paused as Sandra walked in the door carrying two large grocery bags close to her chest. "Sandy's friends with everyone in town. She can get people to open their wallets."

"What's this?" Sandra said warily as she set the bags on the table. "What are you signing me up for now, Tom?" She pushed her long braids back off her shoulders and gave a quick wink to Nate. "I haven't even had a cup of coffee yet."

"I'm planning a 5K to raise money for a new roof, and Tom said you were training to win it."

"Oh, hell no. You're funny." Sandra laughed, and the sound rippled through the space. She lifted two quarts of milk out of one of the bags. "So Tom roped you into planning our road race, is that right?"

"It was his idea," Tom said, palms raised. "I didn't ask him to do anything."

Sandra arched a brow, a knowing look crossing her face. "Yeah, right." She looked at Nate. "You think I'm good at fundraising? This one here is a mad genius. He can convince people it was their idea in the first place."

Tom shrugged before turning and heading toward the back room. "I do what I can."

It was almost eight o'clock. Nate thought if he could get to the Dinardo space early, that might show Mr. Dinardo how interested he was. He hoped it would be enough to convince him to knock thousands off the rent. He turned to Sandy. "I'm going to have to take off. I'll be in touch about the race."

Sandy reached over to press his hand with hers. "Thanks for the help."

Nate folded up the cardboard box he'd emptied and stacked it against the wall with the others. Outside the front door was a small metal locked box marked "Donations." He reached into his wallet, peeled off a few bills, and stuffed them through the slot before heading down the street.

He reached the space with fifteen minutes to spare, but George Dinardo had beaten him. Nate saw him through the glass, removing shelving from the wall behind the counter. He gave a wave when he saw Nate and shuffled to unlock the front door. "Nate Lancaster! Good to see you."

"Mr. Dinardo." Nate accepted his firm handshake. "How's retirement treating you?"

George Dinardo had a shock of white hair, small blue eyes, and rosy cheeks. Nate smiled, remembering a time when all of that white hair had been black. "I'm not retired," Dinardo said with a dismissive wave. "I'm otherwise employed. You know I put a lot of my savings into real estate, right? I own this place outright. This place, and the place next door, and the one next to that. I also have a place over in Spencer. Commercial space on the bottom, some apartments on top. Mixed use."

"I had no idea." Nate was impressed, though. "So you're managing those properties now?"

"You could say that." He sighed. "I've owned this place for almost forty years. Bought it brand new ages ago, back when commercial space cost three dollars," he added with a grin. "The other places I've bought over the last five years, and they all need some work."

"How about this one?" Nate asked, casually stepping closer to look at that water stain on the ceiling. "How's the roof?"

"Roof's fine. I just had it replaced five years ago. Put a little paint up there and the ceiling will look good as new." He took the white shelf from the wall and set one end on the floor. "So you're going to turn the space into a gym? I never thought about it like that. I figured another restaurant would come in."

"It's hard to find large open spaces like this. The plumbing in back could be converted to showers, and those walls would come down easily."

"They would," Dinardo agreed, and patted his hand against one. "They're actually pretty flimsy. Just drywall."

"The windows are great, too," Nate continued. "Lots of natural lighting on a corner space like this." He paused. "You know, I came by on Sunday and spoke with the realtor. He didn't give me a price, though."

Without missing a beat, Dinardo said, "Price is thirty dollars a square foot."

Damn. Nate had secretly hoped the realtor had gotten his numbers wrong. He scratched at his temple. "Thirty dollars? No offense, Mr. Dinardo, but that seems awfully high to me."

He paused to study Nate, appearing to mull this remark over. "You'd be able to make that, I'd think. And then some. How much does a gym membership go for these days?"

"I'd want to keep costs reasonable. Don't forget, I'd have to invest in equipment and hire staff." He shook his head. "That kind of rent would leave me starting in a giant hole. Would you consider anything less?"

"I've given this a lot of thought, and I think that's a reasonable price. Besides, this is my retirement income, and it's only been on the market about a week."

Nate stuck his hands in his pockets and nodded. If the space had only been for rent for a week, then Dinardo wasn't going to be open to negotiating the price yet. Maybe he'd change his mind if it sat empty for a few months, or even a year. "I think it's too high, sir. This is Archer Cove, not Great Barrington."

"Try finding a space in Great Barrington this size," Dinardo replied. "I appreciate your thoughts, Nate, but I'm comfortable with that price for now. Why don't you give it some thought and come back if you change your mind."

Nate held out his hand. "I will, sir. I'd ask you to do the same."

George Dinardo smiled. "Always good to see you, Nate. Give my best to your mother."

100

CHAPTER SIX

THE MORNING BROKE with a heavy gray sky, but nothing like that was going to dampen Jessie's spirits. She had a list of flaws that was painful to look at, but everything could be fixed. She was a work in progress, that was all. By the time Quinn was named partner at Emerson & Parker, Jessica Mallory would be a new woman. Practically perfect.

And it started that morning.

She poured herself a bowl of cereal and resisted the urge to add a teaspoon of sugar. When she reached into the refrigerator for the milk and found that she only had a splash left, she wasn't even angry. "Look at me, saving calories," she murmured to herself. At this rate, she'd be fitting into that dress in no time flat.

She leaned against the counter, chewing her dry cereal. "From now on, I'm going to be ambitious," she announced to Prince Travis, who stared back with characteristic disinterest. "Sorry, am I boring you? If you have somewhere else you'd rather be..."

There she went, talking to herself again. Surely this was evidence of her bakery upbringing. Jessie redirected her attention back to her goals and imagined herself achieving them. Losing weight was simple. That was just a matter of food sacrifice. Like, say, eating dry cereal. Easy.

She chewed the mouthful of cereal. Chewed and chewed. Then she swallowed the lump. Jessie set her spoon back into the bowl. Dry cereal was disgusting. It was kind of like eating paste. Maybe she could add some water?

Nope. That only made things worse.

"That's fine," she mumbled to herself as she set the bowl in the sink. "I got a few good bites in, and it's fortified with essential vitamins and minerals." She should be covered.

So long as she didn't buy milk, losing weight would be simple. Starting her own business, however...well, that made her blood run cold. She was not a salesperson. Her chocolates sold through sheer luck, and she was okay with that. But see, that was the sign of a person without ambitions. Quinn was not a person who settled. He worked so hard that he even sacrificed his relationships. *That* was the mark of an ambitious person, and if she wanted him to see how perfectly matched they were, she couldn't afford to be "okay" with anything.

The first thing she needed to do was to work on her sales pitch.

Jessie poured herself a cup of coffee and regarded the silver fox in the corner. Surely her father must have given her *some* sales genes? "You look like a smart guy, Travis," she said. "So I'm gonna play it straight. I've got this computer upgrade that can process information at the speed of light and quadruple your company's productivity. Some folks get nervous about that kind of thing, because let's face it: increased productivity means increased profits, and increased profits mean growth. Lots of folks aren't ready to grow. They fear it. Do you fear growth, Travis?" She tapped her fingernail against the side of her coffee mug as she thought. "Nope. I definitely don't have Dad's genes."

Also, black coffee was gross. She poured it out into the sink.

As she showered and dressed, Jessie thought back to one of those self-help seminars that Wren had dragged her to one Saturday afternoon. The speaker — a bundle of energy in an ill-fitting black suit and a bolo tie — had shouted at them for three hours straight. "You can't make a change if you don't believe it!" He banged on the lectern after each word. "You've got to believe it first."

"Believing it," they'd learned, required the regular use of affirmations. "Make a deposit. One deposit. Two deposits. A hundred deposits a day, right into the self-esteem bank." Here, the speaker darted his hand straight out, then back again, as if he were jabbing his fingertips against self-doubt's throat.

That morning as Jessie walked to work, she made deposits in her self-esteem bank. "I am ambitious," she whispered to herself as she stepped around an abandoned yellow plastic shovel and pail set. "I have a fire burning inside of me."

Which really made her think more of indigestion. Or a sexually transmitted disease. This would take some work. She considered different affirmations. "I am a chocolate mogul," she mumbled as she waited for a school bus to pull through the intersection onto Alden Street. "I am the answer to the chocolate question." Definitely getting closer.

Jessie was still mulling this over a few hours later as she carried trays of bagels to the Archer Cove Inn. She was so lost in thought that she didn't notice the SUV pulling up beside her. "Hey, Jessie."

She didn't even need to turn her head to see the driver — she'd recognized his voice right away. "Nate! Good morning." She smiled.

He was more dressed up than usual, in a light gray sweater and jeans. Normally Nate looked like he was heading down to the track or coming back from a workout. Today he looked kind of *hot*, to be honest. But she didn't think that, because that was a strange thing to think about your boyfriend's best friend.

Ex-boyfriend. But that was only a temporary situation.

He pulled the SUV over to the curb and rolled down the passenger-side window. "You need help with those platters?"

"I'm taking them over to the inn," she explained, which was not really an answer. "Do you have room in the back?" The order was large that day, and her arms were already getting tired.

"Sure."

He climbed out of the vehicle and walked around the front to lift the trays easily from her arms. "You didn't want to take the van?" he said, referring to the bakery's catering van.

"Not when the weather's nice. It's a good excuse to get outside and get some exercise." She twisted her lips. "You probably think walking is boring."

"We can liven it up. I'll drive them over, and you run after the car. Better yet, you run in front and I'll chase you."

"Nathan, you are hilarious," she said with an exaggerated roll of her eyes. "And aren't you up awfully early?" It wasn't even eight thirty yet.

"Just had some errands to run," he said as he set the trays carefully into the back.

"I'm actually glad I ran into you. I could use your help."

"That doesn't sound good." But he grinned as he said it and shut the trunk door. "No offense, but I'm not going to open a baby shower saloon with you. I just don't think it's right for this town."

Jessie raked her fingers through her hair. "You don't let anything go, do you? But listen, we have a two-minute drive to the inn, and I'm going to cram a lot into that space."

"Thanks for the warning." He climbed into the driver's seat and closed the door. "What's going on?"

"I am," she said, pointing to her heart. "I ate my cereal dry this morning, and I drank my coffee black. I'm determined to be the perfect Emerson & Parker wife," she said simply, and smoothed her hands down her skirt. As if to emphasize the point, she added, "I was even practicing my sales pitch on Prince Travis this morning."

"That's not good. What are you selling these days?"

"Computer upgrades." She paused. "I don't know what those are."

"Details. You're just selling them. Should I even ask what that's all about?"

"I figure if I'm going to make a go at owning my own business, I need to know how it's done. Maybe I'll talk to my dad, find out a few tricks of the trade."

Nate fastened his seatbelt and turned the key in the ignition. "Or you could focus on what you're already doing and make a great product."

"Product will get you only so far," she said, sadly. "I just look at all the hours Quinn puts in at the office, right? He's a great lawyer and whatnot, but he's not going to get a promotion without a little gamesmanship. It's just how these things happen. Anyway, I'm working on my diet as part of my self-improvement project. I was hoping we could work on a meal plan. Or some guidelines. I could be flexible."

Nate glanced at her sidelong. "Tell you what: I'll work with you on meal and fitness plans, absolutely free. But there's one condition."

Jessie sucked in a breath. Conditions were scary. "What's that?"

"I'm planning a 5K for the food shelf. I need sponsors and runners."

She exhaled. So he was looking for a charitable donation? Simple! "That's a great cause. You can count on me." Jessie reached over to pat his hand. "Just let me know the different levels of sponsorship. You know Uncle Hank always contributes —"

"No." The car slowed as it reached the gravel drive leading to the inn. "I need sponsors *and* runners. Two in one."

Her stomach clenched, and she suddenly felt ill. "You want me to...oh, no."

"That's right. You want personal training with yours truly? That's what we're going to work on."

"How many miles is a 5K? Six?"

He smiled. "Close. It's three point one miles."

Good heavens. "That's n-not fair," she stammered. "I'm the client! Don't I set the goals?"

"Seems completely fair to me," he said, pulling the vehicle to a stop in front of the inn. "So what do you say? Oh, and by the way, I'm heading to the country club this afternoon. A buddy of mine runs the activities there." He made a show of checking his fingernails. "I seem to recall you saying something about — what was it? Country club manners?"

Ugh, this was so not fair of him — to turn her objectives against her like that. She groaned and set her head back against the seat so she could stare straight up at the ceiling. "Yes. I need country club manners." Those had been her exact words, in fact.

"Think about the networking opportunities. I can get you access to the country club. And I can get you in shape. But you've got to stretch your comfort zone. That's the price."

Jessie's hands were clenched into tight fists against her thighs. Running a road race? Pros: she would probably get into great shape, and it was for charity. Cons: she could very well die trying.

Damn it. Vanity and charity were going to win.

"Fine," she said through gritted teeth. "I'll train for a...road race." Just saying it made her queasy.

"All right then." He grinned. "We start tomorrow morning. Five a.m."

"I'm out the door at five," she said. "We have to run at four."

Seeing the blood drain from his face was revenge enough. Then he recovered. "Four. No problem. Morning runs are invigorating."

"Fabulous." Jessie's seatbelt was unfastened and she had one foot out the door. "Thanks for the ride! I can take it from here."

"C'mon, I might as well help you carry —"

"No, I've got it." She said it in a cheerful but firm voice and swung open the back door. "You should go back to doing whatever you were doing."

More conversation with Nate could lead to him having more great ideas, and she didn't think she could handle it. She'd heard about gyms that forced people to work out by pushing spare tires around. God help her if

Nate made her attempt that. Jessie was not that kind of girl.

But he wasn't listening to her, and what else was new. When she looked up, he was standing beside the back tire, his hands stuffed in his pockets, watching her without moving. His hair was a little longer than usual, and a lock fell into his eyes. Good thing her arms were loaded with trays, or else she would've reached up and brushed it aside, and then he would've been mortified and probably would've accused her of acting like his mother. But she couldn't help but feel a surge of affection for him at that moment, him and his boyish good looks. Then he read her mind and closed the back door so she didn't have to kick it shut with her foot. She said, "I guess I'll see you tomorrow morning."

He lifted one hand into the air to wave good-bye, and she headed into the inn. She stopped when she reached the doorway and looked over her shoulder. Nate was still there in his SUV, waiting to make sure she made it inside.

Archer Cove Inn was a fixture in the seaside town. Upscale and tastefully decorated with small round vases filled with fresh tulips, inviting couches upholstered in linen, and pillows in soft shades of sea blues and greens, the lobby always gave Jessie decorating inspiration. She thought the stately inn was most beautiful at night, when guests flocked to the sweeping front porch to enjoy live music and drinks across candlelit tables. She often wondered what it would feel like to be one of them: a woman in a beautiful cocktail dress, an adoring partner watching her every move. It was all terribly romantic.

The moment she stepped inside the lobby of the inn, Jessie was greeted by a vision of white and platinum blonde. Anna Tumblesby, the innkeeper, was rushing forward, arms extended. "Tell me you brought chocolate!"

Jessie gratefully unloaded a tray of bagels into Anna's arms. "Just bagels. Are you running low? I can stop by later."

"I've been putting truffles out for cocktail hour, and let me tell you: my guests *love* chocolate with their gin gimlets."

Jessie grinned. "I'll have an emergency delivery to you before cocktails tonight."

"Thank goodness."

Jessie followed Anna past the front desk and down a light blue hall decorated with white wainscoting and small wrought-iron wall sconces. At the end of the hall they reached a room with two walls of windows and a stone fireplace. Outside the windows were hydrangea bushes that were just starting to sprout green leaves. By the high tourist season, they would be bright green and decorated with large bulbs of blue flowers. Beyond the hydrangeas was a stretch of green lawn and an unobstructed view of the ocean. When guests left reviews of the inn, this was the room they mentioned, almost without fail.

Anna had set a series of round tables for brunch, decorating them with white linen tablecloths and vases of fresh-cut lilacs. Jessie had been making deliveries to the inn for so many years that she didn't need any instruction. Bagels went on the long table set up against the far wall, right in the middle.

"These look delicious, as always," Anna gushed as she removed the plastic wrap. "I always receive compliments, and I tell them to stop at Hedda's Bakery on the way home."

"Thanks, Anna. We appreciate that."

"After what you all did for me?" Anna shook her head, fluttering her long blonde curls. "You and your uncle are saints. This is the least I can do."

Last November, Anna had slipped on a patch of ice and broken her ankle. Jessie and Uncle Hank had fully assumed her meal preparation duties for weeks, catering full breakfasts so that Anna's guests wouldn't know the difference. They did it because it was the right thing to do, that was all. Neighbors should help each other. Jessie's cheeks grew warm and she looked away, embarrassed by the compliment. "I should head back. Uncle Hank was busy when I left."

"Go right ahead, honey. Don't let me keep you. Oh, before I forget! Someone was asking after you. Not you, specifically, but your chocolates."

"Really?" Jessie hesitated. "What did they say about them?"

"She wanted to know where I found them, and I said you were a local girl and a one-woman operation." Anna straightened a glass carafe of orange juice. "I get a lot of inquiries about that. You might want to consider expanding."

"It's funny you say that, because I was just thinking about it." She put her hands in her pockets. "But the cost, Anna. I have to find a storefront and buy equipment —"

"That's all easy enough to fix. You get a business loan," Anna replied, setting one hand on her hip. "How do you think I fixed this place up? The front porch was a hurricane away from falling into the ocean when I took over."

Jessie stopped. "Huh." Of course. Why hadn't she thought of that? She suddenly felt a burst of optimism. "Thank you, Anna. That is a wonderful idea."

Anna waved her hand. "Honey, I've got plenty of them. You just come back any time and I'll tell you everything that's wrong with the world and how to fix it."

Jessie smiled. She didn't doubt that was true.

"I'm going to get a business loan," Jessie announced to Emily as they were closing for the afternoon.

Emily was wearing her long brown hair in a braid that she'd rested over one shoulder. The effect was very romantic, but she was scrubbing at the floor with a little brush while wearing yellow gloves that extended to her elbows, which kind of ruined the entire thing. "You're getting a loan today?"

"I'm going to apply for one. I wasn't going to, but I think that I need to be realistic. If I want to strike out on my own, then I need to make sure I'm properly capitalized." The importance of capitalization was something Quinn went on about all the time. "I don't think it should be a big deal, though. Getting the loan, I mean."

"I think it's very brave of you to take that risk and open your own shop. I don't know that I'd be able to do it. I'd probably only get approved for a loan from the Bank of Mom and Dad."

Jessie went silent as she counted the money from the till. Her Bank of Mom and Dad was *so* closed. They were barely a part of her life. Sure, she heard from them. They called weekly — more or less — but otherwise they were too busy. That's why she'd come to live with Uncle Hank and Wren, because her parents were going to be moving to Germany for a few years for her dad's work, and they felt Jessie would be better off staying behind. A few years turned into most of high school and college, and then when they finally returned to the United States, they'd moved to Colorado for a few years before settling in the neighboring town of Spencer. Sometimes it bothered her a lot that her parents had basically abandoned her. Often she didn't even think about them, because it's hard to miss people who are never there.

She shuffled the money from the register into a bank deposit bag and zipped it shut. "I'll take the deposit with me. Be back soon." Uncle Hank would need help preparing for the next day, but he wouldn't miss her if she snuck out for a little while.

The First Bank of Spencer was a short block from the bakery, and Jessie had been going there for so long that she knew all the tellers. Sherry gave her a big smile as she approached the window. Her hair was rusty orange again, recently colored. "How are you doing today, Jessie?"

"Great. I have a deposit, and I was hoping to speak with someone about a business loan."

"I'm sure Mr. White can sit down with you. He's just finishing up with a customer."

"Super."

Jessie folded her hands patiently and waited while Sherry processed the deposit. This really was such a nice, friendly bank. Practically family. In a way, she kind of <u>was</u> borrowing from the Bank of Mom and Dad. Sort of.

Sherry smiled and pushed the bag and deposit slip across the counter. "You're all set, Jessie. You can sit right in that seat over there, and Mr. White will be right out."

"Thanks."

There was no need to feel nervous, but her palms were a bit clammy. She swept them down the front of her skirt as she took a seat in an oddly patterned purple-and-mauve chair. Were the circles on the fabric supposed to be bubbles? She considered the question for a bit. Beside her was a round wooden table on which a series of brochures was fanned out invitingly. Her eyes glazed over at the titles. Securities, trust instruments, blah blah. Banking was so painfully dull. How could anyone even stand this stuff?

"Are you waiting for me, Jessie?"

In her mind, Fred White had always seemed miscast as a loan officer. He should really have been a middle school math teacher, what with his reddish, thinning hair and his friendly eyes. She'd never seen him wearing

114

anything but striped, button-down short-sleeved shirts and khakis in varying shades of clay. He favored earth tones.

"Hi, Mr. White." She rose eagerly to her feet. "Yes, I'd like to talk with you about a business loan, if you have a few minutes."

He waved her into his office, and she took a seat on another ugly chair. She folded her hands in her lap and reminded herself not to slouch. She was applying for a business loan, and that required her to exude confidence.

"Is this a loan for the bakery?" He rounded the large wooden desk, which was equipped with a black blotter, a computer, a cup with three pens, and nothing else.

"It's for a new business I'm starting, actually. I'm thinking I'll call it 'The Chocolate Crush.'" She flashed her fingers for effect.

If she'd been hoping he'd imagine the possibilities with her, Jessie was disappointed. "So you'd sell chocolate bars?"

The lack of enthusiasm was crushing. Would they even be able to conduct a conversation at this rate, above the sound of her heart breaking? "It's so much more than a place to sell chocolate bars, Mr. White. I make my own chocolate. Well, I buy the chocolate wholesale. Belgian chocolate. It comes in these forty-pound bars. I should've brought samples. Would you like me to run back and bring some —?"

He held up his palm. "That's all right. It's not part of the loan application."

He smiled, so it must have been a joke. Ha.

Jessie clasped the hem of her skirt and wound it tightly around her finger while he pulled some forms from a desk drawer. She reached for a pen. "Do you want me to fill those out here, or can I bring them back?"

His mouth quirked upward. "You'll need to bring these back with the accompanying documentation. Our loan officers will need to see a business and marketing plan, projected growth...it's all in the paperwork."

"Uh huh." Jessie chewed on her bottom lip as he slid the paperwork toward her. It was a lot more involved than she'd appreciated. "So for marketing, I've been doing mostly word-of-mouth because I find that's really the best kind. I've worked with Anna Tumblesby, who owns the inn? And she uses my chocolates as part of her turndown service. She puts them on the pillows and everything."

It was like she couldn't stop talking, and she was almost certain she wasn't helping anything. Mr. White looked downward, and she followed his gaze to her skirt, which she'd twisted and pulled into a mess. "Sorry," she muttered as she smoothed it out again, not sure to whom she was apologizing.

"So your chocolates are featured," he said, "as part of the turndown service at the local inn?"

Well, when he put it that way, it didn't sound very impressive at all. "Yes, and a lot of times guests will come by Hedda's and buy a box of chocolates as they're leaving town, you know?"

But judging by the blank look on his face, Mr. White didn't know. At all. She inched closer, setting her knees against the back of the desk and bringing her hands up to rest on top, as if she were pleading with him to understand. "You see, Anna likes my chocolates —"

"Yes, yes. I hear you." He pressed the paperwork into a pile. "This loan application will require a full plan, including market penetration, growth strategies, and the background of the officers of your corporation."

"Officers of my corp —" She stopped. "It's just me. I'm it."

"Uh huh. And you're using this loan to purchase equipment, I assume?"

She scratched one finger against the side of her head. "I was thinking that I'd mostly need it to cover rent for the first year and just get, you know, started." She swallowed. "You — you do that sort of thing, right? Give businesses money to get started? It's a woman-owned business, if it helps —"

Mr. White sighed with excessive patience, and Jessie tucked her hands under her thighs, feeling like a kid in the principal's office. "Ms. Mallory," he started. (So now she was Ms. Mallory? Just great.) "I have to be honest. The kind of loan you're looking for isn't easy to obtain these days. Banks have been much more conservative about lending. Do you have a business plan? A growth plan? Do you have a record of industry success?"

"Yes. Okay. That makes sense." She had none of those things. "My chocolates are really good —"

"Well. Think about it. In the meantime, here's the paperwork you'll need to fill out. I'll put it into a folder for you."

"Great. Thanks."

She left his office clutching a manila file filled with loan papers she was confident she couldn't complete without forming some deal with the devil. *I am the conqueror of setbacks. I hurdle over disappointments.*

On the way out of the bank, she grabbed a lollipop from a bowl and tore off the wrapper. Lime. Just her luck.

With a sigh, she tossed the candy into the trash and headed back to the bakery.

CHAPTER SEVEN

RULE NUMBER ONE: there was no crying in business. It was undignified, and Jessie still had some of her dignity hanging by a thread. She, Emily, and Uncle Hank were huddled around the stainless-steel counter, reviewing the loan application in the kitchen at Hedda's. Even though she was increasingly certain she would never, ever be able to manage to cull together an application that wouldn't get her laughed at, she would not cry. See rule number one.

Emily was leaning forward against the counter, picking at a sticky bun as she considered the documents Jessie had spread out. She lifted a piece of paper and squinted at it. "Do you have articles of incorporation? Or a management team?"

"No. I don't even..." Jessie carefully pried the paper from Emily's fingers. Greasy fingerprints would make her look unprofessional, too. "Uncle Hank, where do I get articles of incorporation?"

"You have to create a business," he said simply, as if that explained everything.

"So, like...can I get that online?"

Uncle Hank was a former Wall Street attorney who, from what she'd pieced together, had experienced a relatively early midlife crisis or minor breakdown and left it all behind to purchase the bakery. Aunt Lilliana had not taken the news well, and they had divorced soon after moving to Archer Cove. Of course, that was all water under the bridge these days, as Auntie Lil and Uncle Hank were very much in love again. No wonder, what with Auntie Lil's impeccable style and grace and Uncle Hank's classic good looks. When they dressed up and went out, they looked like a couple that had walked off some kind of society pages. It was like they'd been made for each other all along, but it had taken them years to realize it.

Auntie Lil had just stopped by the kitchen with a stack of ice-blue handmade linen-blend napkins that she had designed specially for the bakery. She was folding them into neat stacks at the other end of the counter. "Hank," she said in that cool voice of hers, "I think you should explain to Jessie how to create a business entity. It's simple, honey. I created one for The Space Lift," she added, referring to her interior design business. "Wren and Jax run the vineyard under a few different corporate identities."

Uncle Hank leaned his back against the countertop. He was still wearing his favorite apron: white with blue stripes and the word "Dad" stitched on the front in red thread. Wren had given it to him for Father's Day one year. "You have to go on the secretary of the state's website. You make sure your business name isn't taken already, and then there are some forms to fill out and some fees to pay. That's about it."

"And then I'll have everything I need to apply for a business loan?"

Uncle Hank's lips thinned, which could only mean that he was about to deliver some bad or serious news. "Based on these forms, it's an involved process. I can help you with it, but you need to think about how you're going to grow your business. Are you going to offer online sales, or brick and mortar only? How are you going to manage growth?"

Jessie slumped onto a stool and rested her chin on her hand. Here she'd started her day so hopeful, and everything about this conversation was killing her buzz. "I just kind of wanted to sell my chocolates. How do people open businesses, anyway? Are these loans that impossible to get?"

His eyes softened. "You know you're welcome to use the space here. You have full use of the display out front. Customers like your chocolates. All it takes is the right person finding you."

She knew he was right, but it still felt so random. "I don't like the idea of waiting for someone to find me," she said. "I want to control my own life."

"Spoken like a true entrepreneur," he said, and gave her a kiss on the top of her head. "You'll figure it out."

It felt nice for someone to believe in her, and Jessie basked in that warmth for a few minutes before scooping up the loan application and setting it back into the folder. The application was like any recipe: one step, one ingredient at a time, a little technique, and a lot of patience. She'd do well to remember that, and not overcomplicate things.

Jessie hadn't looked at her phone all afternoon. When she finally did, she saw that her mother had called. Five times. Was she on fire?

Jessie dialed the number as she walked home that evening. When her mother picked up, she sounded like she'd been sprinting. "Hello?"

"Hey, Mom," Jessie said. "I saw you called a few times. Is everything okay?"

"Oh, thank heavens you're all right. I was worried sick."

There she went, thanking heaven again. *Blessed be!* Jessie couldn't decide whether she was touched by her mother's concern or disturbed, but she was leaning toward the latter. "I was at work, that's all." She paused. "What did you think happened to me?"

"Ah. Well." There were a few beats of silence and some shuffling.

"Mom? Are you dancing? Did you hear me?"

"I heard you, honey. This is delicate. I heard about Quinn, and I wanted to check in to see how you were holding up. I was fearing the worst."

The worst? What would that be, exactly? Jessie frowned at the sidewalk as she considered the possibilities. "Please don't tell me you thought I'd actually kill myself over Quinn."

Another long pause. "Well, you can be dramatic."

Jessie dropped the phone to her side and counted to ten. When she lifted it again, Sadie was still trying to explain herself."— made me watch this news report. I never should have watched it. I've been sick with worry all afternoon. You don't know anyone on designer drugs, do you? Of course you don't," she added quickly. "What am I thinking? I get these thoughts and I get anxious about things."

"Hmm. Maybe you could do more gardening now that the weather is warm?"

"I think that's a nice idea, Jessie. I could be in touch with nature. It's a form of meditation, very soothing." She hesitated for a moment before she said, "If you want to talk about anything, I'm here for you. I wanted you to know that. I'm trying to be more available now that we live closer."

It wasn't the first time they'd had this conversation, so it didn't come as any surprise to Jessie that her mother had some guilt over abandoning her in high school. Which was really the worst thing that had ever happened to Jessie. It had all turned out all right, she supposed, and Wren and Uncle Hank and even Auntie Lil had been her family during those years. But being dropped off at the bakery had left a raw spot that had never fully healed. How does one get over being the kid whose parents moved to Europe and left her behind? She had an issue or two to work out in that arena.

She took a deep breath just as she passed a lilac bush in full bloom. The heady scent returned her to the present. Maybe her heart still hurt here, but she was working toward healing. There was no need for her to relive past slights. "I don't want you to worry about me, Mom," she said, softly. "I promise I'm not going to do anything drastic — okay? Actually, I'm going to be better than ever."

Her mother's sigh crackled through the phone. "I'm relieved to hear that. But Jessie? I can't help but worry about you. That's how it is when you love someone. You want the best for them." In the background, Jessie heard a male voice. "Your father says hi."

"Tell my father I said hi back."

Sadie's voice was muffled as she said, "Jessie says hi." She returned to the phone. "You call me if you need anything. Are you all set with groceries? Do you need any milk or eggs? I saw an ad for a buy one, get one on pints of strawberries if you need those."

Her heart softened at the offers. "Thanks, Mom. I'm fine. I'll see you soon, okay?"

Nate couldn't sleep for a long time. His stomach was on fire as he waited for the next morning's run. He must have drifted off to sleep at some point, but his mind never quieted. When the alarm went off at three thirty in the morning, he rolled over with a grumble. Then he

124

remembered he was helping Jessie to train for a 5K. Right.

A quick shower to wake up, then he pulled on a T-shirt, shorts, and a college sweatshirt that had seen plenty of better days. He wondered if he was going to have to pull Jessie out of bed. Could he actually be that lucky?

We're running together. He clutched that thought like a paper-thin seashell, hesitant to hold on too eagerly. She could change her mind or twist her ankle. This could be the first and only run. But Nate didn't want to think like that when he was about to introduce Jessie to his favorite sport. Life was good.

He imagined her blonde hair in a ponytail, her blue eyes bright, working up a healthy sweat beside him. He hoped he could hold it together, be a professional. This was going to require more effort than usual. He'd have to treat her like any client, not get overly excited or — God forbid — aroused. Even though Jessie wasn't like any client he'd trained, then or ever. Because he'd never been in love with a client.

Dawn was just breaking, and the sky was a light shade of dove gray. She opened her door when he pulled up in the SUV, then shut it behind her and gave him a little wave. So much for his fantasy of pulling her out of bed. "Ready?"

Damn, she was perky even at four in the morning. He'd have to get whatever coffee she drank. "The question is, are *you* ready?" he said as he climbed out of the vehicle and shut the door behind him. "Because I'm about to kick your ass into shape."

125

Jessie wrinkled her nose. "You men always make everything so violent. How about, you're about to gently lead me down the path of fitness?"

She smiled that brilliant smile that lit up her face and took his breath away. His collar tightened. Not a stellar start to a professional session. "How about this: I'll kick your ass gently? You'll be sore tomorrow, but you'll love it."

She tilted her head at him. "A gentle ass-kicking, huh? I guess I'll take it."

She was wearing tight gray leggings that ended mid-calf and — man! — did a lot of favors for her glutes. As he approached, she reached her arms overhead, exposing a small stretch of bare skin around her abdomen. A very nice abdomen it was. He unzipped his sweatshirt a few inches, feeling hot around the collar, and reminded himself to *be a professional, God damn it.*

"Should we stretch first, or what?" She set her hands on her hips and tilted her neck from side to side.

"We'll stretch at the end," he said. That was assuming he could exhaust himself so he wouldn't pop an erection at the sight of her working out tight muscles. "Let's start by walking."

She shrugged. "Okay."

"You're going to have to get running shoes, first of all. Those things on your feet don't have enough support."

He saw by the look on her face that he'd just broken her heart. "But I love these shoes!"

Of course she loved them, because they were bright purple with pink laces. "Yeah, they're great-looking. But they don't have any cushioning. Head to Fast Tracks. They'll measure your feet and check your gait and everything."

"Check my gait?" She groaned. "It's way too early for this."

"I don't want you sidelined by shin splints. Remember, this is for charity."

He'd trained plenty of clients for their first 5K. The distance was friendly — just a little over three miles — but challenging enough to be a real achievement. His greatest professional rewards came at the finish lines of local races when he saw the sheer exuberance on his clients' faces.

He glanced over at Jessie to check how she was holding up. She was quieter than usual and rubbing her palms together as they headed down the street. Nervous. He leaned over and bumped her shoulder with his and said, "You've got this. We're going to start slowly, do a little walking, pick it up to a jog for about ninety seconds, and then walk again."

When he'd first started out, Nate had made the mistake of coaching his clients the way he'd want to be coached. Physical activity had always come naturally to him, and he welcomed challenges. He needed to be pushed. But although he trained the occasional triathlete or marathoner trying to qualify for Boston, most of his clients just needed help getting back into shape. They needed encouragement, and would fold if pushed too hard. This was the art of it, he supposed.

Besides, he knew a lot about Jessie. When she wanted something, she approached it from every angle until she got it. But this was a new challenge, and he didn't want to reinforce her belief that she wasn't an athlete. He released a breath as they walked in silence, realizing that he'd miscalculated by talking tough. Blame it on the missed hours of sleep. "You're going to push for those ninety seconds, and I want you to feel it tomorrow, but I promise you it will be a good kind of sore, all right? No ass-kicking involved."

The tension in her brow melted and she nodded. "Okay. Thanks."

As they came to the corner stop sign, Nate thought about all the summer mornings he'd run down this very street, across the course he was about to share with Jessie. It was still one of his favorite routes. And he could grow to love this time of the morning, when the air was damp and smelled like last night's cut grass. "We're going to pick up to a jog now. I want you to be able to talk, but not sing. Make sense?"

She pressed her lips together and brushed some stray hairs from her face. "Don't set off without me, please. You're so much faster than I am."

He saw in the wrinkle of her brow how much that fact embarrassed her. He'd been prodding her for years to join him for a run, and he'd always taken her dismissal as a lack of interest. All this time, she'd been afraid she wasn't good enough. "It takes a lot of guts to get out for your first run. You set the pace. I don't judge my clients — or my friends. Start whenever you're ready."

She took a deep breath and set off. He followed, making sure to allow her to lead, if only by inches. They wound through the neighborhood, down the little side streets with gardens and picket fences. He felt nostalgic. When he was a kid, middle-class families could still afford to buy a vacation cottage by the shore, and they had. He'd lived on the other side of Archer Cove with his parents and brother and sister, but he'd spent summers here in his grandmother's cottage, playing with his summer friends who lived in New York for the rest of the year. Now the properties had changed hands a few times with every boom in the market. The neighborhood had become a revolving door for tourists and investors. He missed the old days, when he could pair homes to families.

They ran a cycle in silence, and as they started to walk, Jessie said, "My mom called me last night. She called me a few times while I was at work, and when I didn't answer, she assumed I'd jumped off a bridge. Because of Quinn."

Nate eyed her. "She thought that? Literally?"

"*Literally*. It's like, my parents moved to Germany for almost four years and left me behind, then they moved out to Colorado and left me behind. Now that they're close by, they want to be involved in my life, but they don't even know who I am."

He turned that over for a moment. She'd never opened up to him about her parents before, and he could practically hear the old injury in her voice. "They let you down, didn't they?"

He thought he knew how she felt. His father had died of brain cancer when Nate was thirteen, and he'd spent a long time feeling abandoned. It had taken years of therapy for him to begin to understand it, and he still didn't know if he did. He only knew that life was precious, and painful, and beautiful, often all at the same time.

"Yeah, they let me down," Jessie said. "I spent a lot of time thinking they must not have wanted me around. How could they have, if they left?" She glanced down at his watch as it beeped. "Time to run?"

"Yeah. Let's go."

They set off again. This time, Jessie ran harder, almost as if she were chasing something down. Or running away from it. When they walked again, she kept the conversation light, and he didn't venture back to her parents.

After several cycles, they ended right where they'd begun, at the stop sign. The morning sun had broken by then. "Done," he announced. "How do you feel?"

She was covered with a light sheen of perspiration, and her hair was disheveled. Her cheeks were light pink. It was almost unbearably sexy. "Good," she puffed as she caught her breath. She bent over, setting her hands on her thighs, and eyed him sidelong. "You're not even out of breath."

"Jess. This is my job. I work out with people all day."

"Still. I'm like, dying here." She choked out a laugh and swept the back of her hand across her forehead. "I was thinking," she said, in between gasps. "You should open...your own gym...I mean it. You'd be...so great at that, and you could...keep better hours and everything."

"Maybe one day." Nate thought back to his conversation with Dinardo. Until the rent came down, opening a gym wasn't an option. "What about you? Are you working on your chocolate shop?"

"I have a few ideas. I think the right thing will come along. I'm going to take charge of what I can, you know?" She set her hands on her hips. "Hey. Thanks for listening to me complain. I didn't mean to dump on you like that."

"It's okay. You'd be amazed at what my clients tell me when we run. It's like it opens people up."

She nodded and took a few more breaths. "I've got about five minutes before I need to get ready for work. Are you going to help me stretch out?"

His collar tightened at the thought of working out her hamstrings in those tight pants. He tugged his sweatshirt lower to hide the evidence. "Yeah. Let's go."

There were daffodils sprouting outside the front door of the little blue cottage. One couldn't be pessimistic around sprouting flowers. And then when Jessie came to the bakery, there was a large order of chocolate waiting for her.

Uncle Hank pulled two pans of his almost-famous coffee cake from the oven and set them on the counter.

"Are you running out of work space? We can try moving some of the bakery equipment around."

She licked her tongue into the corner of her mouth as she considered the question. She had two marble slabs now and a machine that tempered chocolate, and then the rack that held the candy molds. Things *were* getting a bit tight, weren't they? "Sorry, Uncle Hank. I placed a larger order this time because the candy's been selling. I won't do that again."

"No, see, that's not what I wanted to hear." He set down the large red oven mitts and walked across the kitchen toward her. "I'm glad your chocolates are selling, and I want you to sell even more. We just need to figure out how we can make that happen." He paused. "I don't have a tenant for upstairs yet. Do you want to store some of these bars there?"

Upstairs was the three-bedroom apartment she'd only recently vacated. Auntie Lil had redecorated the space, torn down the old wood paneling, and generally modernized the unit, but Uncle Hank had to replace some of the appliances before renting it out. "Great idea," she said. "It's only temporary, though, so if you need me to get out of there —"

He waved a hand. "Don't worry. It works for now."

They each made a few trips, carrying the forty-pound chocolate bars up the back stairs into the apartment unit. By the time they were finished, they had relieved some of the congestion. At least, Jessie had enough floor space to actually work.

Customers had been requesting toffee, of all things, and she was running low. That morning she devoted time to making several batches. She also made a batch of hazelnut crème truffles and dark chocolate raspberry swirl hearts. By lunchtime, she was feeling downright productive. *When chocoholics call, I appear.*

She changed her apron and stepped into the main bakery to help Emily with the lunch crowd, which was always a little daunting. She ran orders from the tables while Emily processed the to-go line. It got so busy that she didn't even notice when Nate arrived. He was visiting with a very tall, very muscular man, and she wasn't quite sure how long they had been sitting at the table in the corner.

"Gosh, I'm so sorry," she said as she darted over, shaking her head and pulling a pencil from behind her ear to take their orders. "I hope you haven't been waiting long."

"We just got here," Nate said good-naturedly, but then he was probably stretching the truth a little. "Jess, do you remember Max Castonguay? He may have moved out of Archer Cove before you moved in."

"I don't believe we've met," Max answered for her, and rose to shake her hand. "It's a pleasure."

"Nice to meet you," she said. He had to be well over six feet tall, and he looked like he spent all day working out. "Are you a personal trainer like Nate?"

"Navy SEAL," he said, pulling back his shoulders just slightly. "Just back for a couple weeks, visiting my folks."

133

"Oh. Well, welcome, and thank you for your service." She positioned the pencil over the pad. "What can I get —"

"I was telling Nate here that he's too soft on his clients," Max continued. "Life's about pushing limits."

Jessie and Nate shared a glance, and Nate broke into a smile. "You're cut from a different cloth, Max. If I told my clients to work out until they puked, I wouldn't have many of them."

"I disagree. You'd be known for getting results." Max sat back in his chair and leaned back, stretching his long legs. "It's about making them tough here," he said, pointing to his head. "You push to the brink of death, but no further."

Nate lifted his eyebrows and glanced at Jessie, who was standing with pencil poised and jaw dropped, staring in disbelief at the newcomer. "How about it, Jess?" he said. "I'm going to adopt that training philosophy, and you're going to be my guinea pig."

"Do you work out?" An interested smile tugged at Max's lips. "We could go out later."

Jessie blinked and shook her head. "Uh, no. My workout is mostly running lunch orders. Speaking of which, today we have a great chicken salad —"

"I've finally convinced Jessie to train with me," Nate said, leaning forward across the table. "Maybe she'd prefer someone tougher."

Now he was teasing her. She tilted her head at Nate and shot him her best warning look, but Max was undeterred. "It's all mental," he said, poking at his head with his index finger. "If you want to run a marathon tomorrow, you know how it's done? One step at a time. You just gotta commit to keep going. You get a goal in your head and don't let anything stop you."

"Thank you for that," Jessie said softly, and paused to chew on her lip. "I don't think I want to run a marathon."

"She's starting her own chocolate business." Did she detect a hint of pride in Nate's voice? "You should try some."

"I definitely will," Max said. His gaze was intense, and she shifted a little to try to avoid it. "You should run a marathon, at least once. But the same lessons apply in life. Hard work and determination. Nothing can stop you unless you let it. Push to the brink of death."

She nodded. "And no further. Got it. Good advice."

"And here you thought you were only taking our lunch orders." Nate sat back in his seat with a satisfied grin on his face, clearly enjoying himself. "We'll both have the chicken salad. On wheat."

"Two chicken salads. Great."

"Make mine rye," Max said. "And hey, the offer stands if you want to work up a sweat later."

"Thanks." She tucked the pencil behind her ear. "You've given me a lot to think about."

She spun in place before Max had a chance to add anything else to the lecture. *I work to the brink of death, but no further.* For some reason, the affirmation didn't inspire her.

Emily was staring at her when she reached the counter again. "What just happened there? You look a little dazed."

"I think Nate's friend just propositioned me. Though he may have been talking about running. Or hard labor."

"Ah." Emily glanced over her shoulder at the two men, who appeared to be engaged in a lively conversation. "Too bad it wasn't Nate."

Jessie was half-listening as she started to prepare their lunch orders. "Pardon?"

"He's hot. Nate, I mean." She leaned back against the counter, flicking the end of her ponytail over her shoulder. "I know you guys are friends. You probably can't even look at him that way, but he's seriously cute."

Jessie felt her forehead tense as she set two thick slices of wheat on a plate and added sliced tomatoes and shredded lettuce. There was no reason in the world it should bother her that Emily thought Nate was hot. She was entitled to her opinion, and jeez, obviously Nate was attractive, and they were both single and everything. Jessie was barely single. Single for now, that was all. She swallowed. "Yeah, for sure."

Emily smiled. "Quinn is hot too," she said. "Definitely. He has that football star thing."

"Mhmm." Jessie bit her lower lip. "Quinn and I recently decided to take a break. He's busy, and I'm busy. We both needed some space."

Emily's eyes grew large, and her hand flew to her mouth. "Oh my gosh, I'm so sorry! I shouldn't have said anything."

136

Jessie put a hand on Emily's arm. "It's fine, really. It was mutual in a way, so don't worry." She glanced over at Nate and Max. "You know, I just realized I forgot to ask them what they wanted to drink. Would you mind running over there?"

Emily bounced away, and Jessie took a moment to collect her breath. When she looked up, she watched Emily chatting up Max and Nate, and both men laughing in response to something she'd said. A pang worked its way through Jessie's stomach. *Low blood sugar, that's all.* She'd forced down a bowl of plain oatmeal that morning and hadn't eaten since. She turned her back on the scene and kept her mind on the work before her.

Her and Nate? Now that would be just strange. He was Quinn's best friend, for one, and sometimes he was seriously annoying. Like when he'd picked her up at the baby shower and teased her about being a nun in a trampy black habit. Although it was nice of him to give her a ride home when she needed it. No denying he was thoughtful, and he was one of those people who was always around when she needed him. Reliable. And a pretty good listener, which was hard to find. But he definitely didn't think of her like that, and if he ever found out that these thoughts had even crossed her mind, he'd probably dunk her head in the toilet.

"Hey, Jess?"

She jumped at the voice and turned to see Nate leaning over the counter. "Y-yes?"

"Can I get a few lemon slices? For our waters," he added.

It took her a moment to snap back to reality. "Oh. Of course." She grabbed a handful of sliced lemons from a container and placed them in a small white ceramic bowl. "Here you go."

"Thanks."

She pressed her lips together and wondered if she'd ever noticed how nice his smile was. "And — oh! I owe you rent! Can I get it to you tonight?"

"It's okay, no rush." He grinned. "I know where you live."

"No, it's almost the middle of the month. I need to pay you."

"I'll stop by later, then."

Jessie pretended not to watch Nate walk away, or to notice how broad his shoulders were, or how muscular his legs. She glanced away to the black-and-white tiled floor, feeling guilty. Some avenues were better left unexplored. Besides, relationships soured, and Nate was a friend too valuable to lose.

CHAPTER EIGHT

JESSIE FLUNG OPEN the cottage windows to admit the soft spring breeze. No doubt about it, everything was better in spring. There was something healthy in change and renewal, and days like this were made to inspire people to do profound things, like write poetry. Or in her case, craft chocolates.

Up that evening: dark chocolate peanut butter fudge. "Don't tell anyone this, but my peanut butter fudge totally sucks," she confided to Prince Travis as she pulled an assortment of ceramic nesting bowls onto the counter. "And that suckiness stops right now." She set her hands on the counter, reigning over the ingredients and tools. "I am master of my destiny," she whispered. "Or mistress. Whatever."

What she was *not* doing that night was thinking about Quinn. No sir. She had a doozy of a project in this peanut butter fudge. Perfecting the recipe, for one. Not eating too much of it, for another. Staying on track would require all of her mental fortitude — and a glass of chardonnay. That was chilling in the refrigerator. "Don't judge me, Travis," she warned as she unscrewed the metal cap and poured a glass. "You don't know what kind of week I've had. It's worth the calories." Besides, she'd only had a cup of fruit salad for lunch.

Her heart had been hurting all day. That dull aching that comes from wanting someone and knowing they don't want you back. Even if she reminded herself that, rationally, she and Quinn had been coming to an end for a long time, that didn't make the inevitable stop any less painful. Breaking up hurt like hell. Being dumped hurt even more. Normally, she'd work late at the bakery, but that evening she wanted to be in the comfort of her own home. She turned on the radio and listened to a Top 40 station, but otherwise she was all business as she measured sugar and butter. This was a distraction she needed.

Jessie reached for the shelf where she kept her cookbooks and removed a shiny silver notebook with the words "Follow your heart" embossed on the cover. This had been a gift from her mom, who'd suggested she start keeping a diary. "Write down your hopes and dreams, and send them to the heavens," her mom had said brightly.

Jessie didn't think she needed to write down her hopes and dreams or send them anywhere. Usually, they were fairly modest. Like, hope to sell enough boxes of truffles to cover rent. Or hope that she didn't slip on something and fall flat on her bottom in front of whatever attractive customer might be in Hedda's. Dream that the rain would hold out until she'd made it home, that kind of thing. So instead, she used the little journal to record her recipes.

The journal was equipped with several silver ribbons that Jessie used as bookmarks. For each experiment, she recorded every ingredient, including the brand name, in addition to the details about amounts and technique. She suspected her peanut butter fudge was failing because she was using the wrong brand of peanut butter. For that night's experiment, she had three different brands to try.

As she drank white wine and hummed along to the radio, Jessie almost completely lost track of time. When she poured the batch of fudge into the pan, she was pleasantly surprised to find that it was only six o'clock in the evening. She would need to allow the fudge to cool for a while, so she picked up her cell phone and called Nate. No harm in trying to butter up her landlord every now and then, especially when she'd been a little bit of a handful lately, what with her crises and all.

He picked up on the second ring. "Hello?"

Her heart skipped at the sound of his voice. Jessie shook it off. "Hey. Want to stop over now and get the rent check? I just made fudge."

"What kind of fudge?"

Jessie sighed as she set the mixing bowls into the sink. "Peanut butter and dark chocolate. Why, are you picky now?"

"I was hoping you made rocky road. If it's only peanut butter, I'll pass."

"Because it's terrible, right?" She groaned. "No, see! I'm experimenting with the recipe, trying to make it better! That's why you have to come over and tell me if I succeeded."

"Stop trying to push your fudge on me, Jessica Mallory."

She smiled as she ran her finger along the inside of the bowl. "Come on. You always know how to make me laugh, and my heart's kind of broken." She'd meant to say it lightly, but then her voice had cracked. That spot in her chest sure hurt. "Fine. Don't come over. I'll just sit here and watch that commercial about the shelter animals over and over, then call you up to cry about it."

"That one with the one-eyed cat? An empty threat." He wasn't buying it, and good for him. He paused momentarily before saying, "All right, I'll be over in a little while. But I swear: if you're watching that commercial, I'm leaving. Understood? No self-pity."

Jessie grinned as she disconnected the call and ran the water to wash dishes. Nate was exactly the right person to call, and she felt better already. By the time he arrived, the kitchen was gleaming again, but the fudge wasn't cooled. Nate groaned in mock exasperation. "You promised me a piece of your shitty peanut butter fudge."

She launched a dishtowel at his head. "What are you talking about? I'd like to see you do any better."

He caught the dishtowel with one hand and calmly set it back on the counter. "You think I drove three blocks to spend time with you? I could be working on my sun salutations."

"Your what now?" Jessie untied her pink polka-dot apron and folded it carefully before placing it back in the drawer beside a pair of matching oven mitts. She'd acquired them months ago, dreaming of the day she'd own a fully-coordinated chocolate shop. If it was strange to want to match her imaginary awning, she didn't care.

"Sun salutations," he replied, and pulled up a stool at the breakfast bar. "Didn't I tell you? I'm teaching yoga at the country club. And no, before you ask, it's not actually on the golf course. Though that would be a great idea and you should raise it with management."

He grinned. Something happened then. Something strange and powerful that went a little like this: Nate looked at Jessie, and Jessie looked at Nate.

Really looked at him.

She took in his green eyes and his perpetually tousled brown hair. She ran her gaze across his finely sculpted face, down his neck, and to the muscular shoulders peeking from beneath his shirt. She noticed for the first time that he had a tiny white line below his lower lip — a fine sliver of a scar — and that was because she was noticing his mouth, which looked quite delicious. For the first time in their years of friendship, Jessie saw Nate for the gorgeous male specimen that he was, and she thought right then that she'd pay cash money to see him run through a few sun salutations, herself. *Yikes and what the hell?*

She was grateful when Nate changed the subject.

"I've also been working on a nutrition plan for you. It's pretty basic, but you happen to work in temptation central, so it could be a challenge."

"No way," she said. "I'm fully committed to this. Wren and Jax are getting married, and I need to lose some weight."

"Sure." Nate nodded. "People normally go on a diet before their cousin gets married. Nothing unusual about that at all. But listen: I talk to my clients all the time about their goals, and I tend to discourage losing weight for a particular event and encourage a more permanent lifestyle change. Weddings are happy events, but maybe not weight loss events."

"Whatever works, I guess." Jessie fluttered her lips and absently lifted a crumb from the counter. "You know, weddings make me feel funny. Through the champagne and the cheese platters and the baked chicken with mushroom sauce, I keep coming back to the fact that the bride and groom are going to have sex that night." She paused. "Do you think I'm a pervert?"

"No, but that must be especially awkward for you at family weddings." Nate leaned over the breakfast bar to get a better look at the fudge. "Is fudge supposed to take this long to set, or is this a hallmark of shittiness?"

She sighed and tapped the pan. "Should be done soon. You want to go for a walk?"

"Love to."

They took a walk down by the pier off Arrow Beach, at the edge of the downtown. The sun was beginning to set, and the office buildings were clearing out for the evening. Nate allowed Jessie to take the lead — her walk, he figured. It didn't surprise him that they wound up in front of Emerson & Parker. He stuffed his hands into his pockets and kicked a small stone in his path. "His car is still here."

She jumped, then recovered quickly. "Whose car?"

"Please." He nodded at the BMW. "Quinn's. Is that why we're here? To see what he's doing?"

Jessie rubbed her head and winced. "I — this looks terrible. I didn't even realize it. I swear."

A likely excuse, but Nate bit his tongue. She'd been single for less than a week, and even if the relationship had been going south since it began, she was probably entitled to be weird for a few days. That didn't mean he had to like any part of it, only that he had to try to keep his irritation in check. "Tell you what. I'll treat you to an ice cream. They have a new flavor —"

"No, remember? I'm on a diet. That's why you're trying the fudge." Her eyes were focused on the door to Emerson & Parker. "I really wasn't thinking about him at all. I mean, this day has been about *not* thinking about him. It's like my own brain is trying to sabotage me."

"Now you sound like some kind of conspiracy theorist." He scratched at his shoulder. He was helping Jessie's subconscious to stalk his best friend. This was awkward. "Fine, if you're on a diet, I'll just buy a cone for myself and you can watch me eat it. We'll need to turn right here." He tugged at her elbow, but she was frozen in place. "Jess, I'm trying to be supportive, and I'm trying not to question the whole 'my subconscious made me do it' excuse, but this is kind of strange —"

"Fudge," she whispered, and turned her face. "That's him, isn't it?"

She pulled closer to Nate, pressing her face almost into his chest and tugging at his shirt with her hands. A thrill darted across his skin at the contact. "I don't — what are you doing?"

"Hiding."

She'd wrapped both arms around his torso and pressed her face into his sternum. It felt pretty nice to have her there, but when he'd imagined their first real date, hiding from Quinn wasn't exactly what he'd had in mind. He didn't even know where to put his hands. He eventually settled on setting them gently on her upper back. "You know that he can still see you, right?"

"Shhh." He felt her inhale before she whispered, "What's he doing?"

Nate lowered his head, trying to conceal his face. His friend was across the street, but not far. All Quinn had to do was look up. Fortunately for him and Jessie, Quinn's interest was somewhere else. Nate's stomach lurched. Quinn was watching the door to E&P, where Caryn had just emerged.

"Nate? What's he doing?"

"Uh, looks like he's checking his phone."

Quinn was in fact watching Caryn intently. She smiled and kissed his cheek. Jessie burrowed her face against him. "He's checking his phone?" He heard a note of panic in her voice. "Is he leaving? I don't want him to see me!"

At that moment, leaving seemed like a great idea to Nate, who definitely didn't need Jessie to see how quickly Quinn had moved on. He turned slightly, angling her away from view. "He's not looking over here. Wait." He ducked his head. "Don't move." Something had suddenly drawn Quinn's interest to their direction.

Jessie's eyes were huge. "Did he see us?" She tightened her grip on his shirt, brushing her fingertips against his skin, but he was hardly going to complain about it.

Now they were locked in some twisted embrace, and Nate had no way of knowing whether Quinn was still watching them. Nate was turned in such a way that he couldn't check behind him in the reflection on the storefront windows. But he sure felt obvious, like their effort at not calling attention to themselves had backfired in a big way. "We can't stay here like this," he murmured into her hair. "We look like we're up to something."

"Shoot." She looked up. "What do we do?"

He couldn't let her see Quinn, that was for sure. Jessie didn't need to mix insult with heartache. He took a breath. "How about this?" Then he pulled her into his arms, and he kissed her.

Her lips were soft and warm, her breath sweet, and she smelled faintly sugary. He was gentle, even tentative as she melted against him. And then suddenly she stood on her toes and pulled his face toward hers with both hands. She was kissing him — *really* kissing him.

Nate's spine stiffened. If this continued much longer, he was going to get aroused, and then he would have a different, very obvious problem. *Oh, what the hell.*

He kissed her back, reaching up to grab a handful of her soft, flowery-smelling hair. She was perfect. Better than perfect, and his heart pounded insistently as if to point it out. Her fingers trailed gently down his arms, tickling his skin until they found his hands. She laced her fingers with his. Nate's chest swelled at the sweetness of the gesture. He pulled her closer to him, savoring the heat of her chest against his.

He lost track of where he was, so that when she finally pulled back and whispered, "Is he gone?," Nate had to stop and remember who she was talking about. Oh, right. Quinn.

Quinn could go to hell.

Nate released a long, slow breath and looked over his shoulder. If Quinn saw them, so be it. He knew that Quinn wouldn't care if Nate was kissing Jessie. In his friend's mind, he'd already moved on. Or back, or wherever. If Quinn was there, watching them, maybe that wouldn't be so bad. Jessie would finally learn the truth, and he'd take her out for a beer so she could cry about it, and then they could all get on with their lives. But although Nate squinted his eyes against the glare off the ocean, he didn't see Quinn. Or Caryn. The BMW was gone, too.

"They left," he said.

Immediately, she released her grip on his shirt. "Thank goodness." She paused, her hands still loosely clutching his shirt. "Wait. Who's 'they'"?"

Nate's mouth went dry as he realized his slip. "I meant 'he.'" Quinn. Sorry."

"Oh." She inhaled a shaky breath, drawing her hand to her heart. "Oh my gosh, I was so afraid he would see me." She giggled.

Nate didn't see what was so damn funny about it. "What would be the problem if he saw you? We're out on a walk. He doesn't own this section of town."

She finger-combed her hair down. "I didn't want him to think I was following him. Really, I hadn't even thought about that. I just like to walk down here. I guess I wasn't thinking."

Her heart was in full-on panic mode, fluttering like a frightened bird. Nate had kissed her, and she'd kissed him back. She'd stuck her tongue in his mouth! Her first thought was that Nate was a genius. He knew that Quinn wouldn't look if he saw two people kissing on the sidewalk. Maybe he'd keep moving. So she'd just shut off her brain and gone for it, figuring Nate would completely understand, and maybe he'd even think that was the only appropriate response under the circumstances. Possibly she hadn't been thinking much whatsoever. It was likely she'd lost her damn mind.

But the kiss wasn't the problem. Her heart wasn't sputtering because of Quinn, but because of Nate.

Because they'd kissed, and she'd liked it, and that felt kind of confusing. He'd no doubt give her a wedgie just to make it clear where they stood.

She swallowed and forced a laugh from her throat. "The kiss was a brilliant idea, by the way. Sorry that I totally probed your mouth! I'm so sorry about that. I just figured Quinn wouldn't look at us, but I should've asked your permission before, you know. Probing." She laughed and tucked her hair behind her ears. "Consent is important, and we were just pretending. I should've kept it theatrical."

Why was he looking at her that way, with that unreadable stare? Was he angry or something? "Nate? I'm sorry. We're not dating, and it was a stupid thing for me to do. Are we still friends? I don't want things between us to be weird."

He winced slightly, then turned his face away. "You kissed me back because of Quinn?"

Boy, was she stepping into something messy. She tugged at the ends of her hair with both hands. "I don't know why I did it. I panicked, and you know how sometimes I act without even thinking, like my mind goes blank —"

"It's not right." He pushed his hands into his pockets and turned away from her. "It's not right."

He was silent for a long stretch, during which she searched for the right words to make the situation a little less horrible. But then Nate interrupted her thoughts by muttering, "Come on. I'll walk you home."

"I thought you wanted ice cream?"

"I changed my mind."

He took a few steps away from her while she stood there, frozen in place, pulling at her hair. "Wait! I said I was sorry. Nate. Talk to me."

He halted his steps and she caught up, feeling flustered and disheveled. When she met his gaze, it wasn't cold or angry. It was more sad. "How long did you date Quinn?"

"Three months." Ten weeks and five days, to be exact, but he'd think she was bizarre for counting like that. "Why?"

Nate reached up to rub the back of his neck. "And for how many of those months would you say things were actually good? I mean, all you've done for weeks now is complain that Quinn is working late and doesn't have time for you. You said that he didn't want to commit or get serious. What kind of boyfriend does that?"

"That's not fair. He's been working hard."

Nate tilted his head in a way that made her wonder what she was missing. "You make a lot of excuses for him."

She knew what he wanted her to say, but her heart hurt just then, and she realized that she wasn't ready to stop making those excuses yet. She swallowed a lump in her throat. "I know I do. But Quinn and I are only taking a break for a little while. He has to figure out some things first." She reached out and found his hand. "I'm sorry. It's hard to explain."

His fingers wouldn't lace with hers. He was staring at her with a pained expression, like he had a million thoughts he wasn't telling her about. Though to be fair, she had a few thoughts of her own. It was time to change the subject. "So, we can make a lunch date at the country club, right? And we'll drink fancy iced tea and do yoga on the ninth hole?"

He looked down at their hands then as if noticing them for the first time. "You've created this entire self-improvement project as a way to win Quinn back. You want to change yourself for him."

Jessie dropped his hand. "Not entirely. This is mostly about me learning how to become more sophisticated. If I'm going to be a successful career woman, I need to act the part."

She felt a twinge of guilt, lying to him like that. Mostly, Jessie wanted to go to the country club to network with the other E&P wives. She could be charming, and maybe they'd go back to Quinn and tell him how foolish he'd been to break up with her. But Nate would not support that plan. She cleared her throat. "It's networking. I can tell people there about my chocolates and maybe find a few investors."

Nate didn't look convinced, but he released a long sigh before saying, "We'll set up a time."

He began walking again, and Jessie bounced along behind him. "Are you sure you don't want ice cream?"

"Yeah, I'm sure."

They walked along in silence. "We're still running tomorrow morning, right? I have my running clothes all washed and ready to go."

"Sure. That's fine."

There was a sudden chill between them, and Jessie wrapped her arms across her chest. Sometimes Nate needed some space, and she understood that. She thought that if they walked for a little while without talking, things would probably be better in a block or two. But when they reached the cottage and Nate still looked sullen, she didn't know what to do. Was he that angry about the kiss, and about her feelings for Quinn?

She was so lost in thought that Nate was halfway out the door before she remembered the real reason she'd initially invited him over. "Oh! I should pay my rent before you evict me."

A weak smile crossed his lips. "You look tired. Get it to me tomorrow."

"After you came all the way over here? Hold on. I'll just be a minute."

He waited by the door while she shuffled around the kitchen, looking for the checkbook that wasn't where it was supposed to be. The perils of living alone, she thought. When you can't find something, there's no one else to blame. Finally she found it in a drawer, pushed to the side by a half-empty box of birthday candles and a tape measure. "Here we are! Just a sec."

She carefully wrote out the check amount and then handed it to him. Nate didn't even look before folding it in half and putting it in his pocket. "Thanks."

"You should take care with that. I have sufficient funds, you know."

The side of his mouth turned up in a half-smile. "For a change. Now go to bed and don't watch animal shelter commercials or think about newlyweds. Nothing good comes of it."

Jessie fired off a salute. "Aye aye."

Before he left, he tried a piece of the fudge and said that it was a better recipe. Jessie broke off a small piece and had to agree that this was an improvement. Still, she could do better.

She turned to the ingredients again. She had time to make another batch before bed, and with a little more sugar, it might be perfect.

As she was melting the chocolate, a realization knocked her against the head. How could she have been so blind? Nate had been single for months, ever since what's-her-name, that girl she'd never thought was good enough for him. All this time, Nate had been watching his best friends date, and that must have been so difficult for him! Just like it was difficult for Jessie to go to Maggie's baby shower and see people close to her getting married and having babies.

She dipped a spoon into the pot of melted chocolate. Nate was lonely. She'd been callous to not recognize that. Well, no longer! He was a great guy, and he deserved to be happy. There was nothing to do but to find the perfect woman for him. Life was like baking, and all one had to do was add the right ingredients in the right order.

She lifted the spoon from the chocolate and considered it. Diet be damned. She ran her finger across the edge and tasted it. Perfection.

CHAPTER NINE

NATE OPENED THE trunk of his car and grabbed the plastic shopping bag. Inside was a pair of brand-new running shoes for Jessie. She'd told him during their run that morning that she'd been measured in the running store, but that she'd need to save up to buy a pair. Nate knew the owner, and he knew the store entered everyone's foot measurements and characteristics into a computer for future reference. Jessie was a size nine with average arches, no pronation issues. Buying her the perfect pair of shoes had taken all of five minutes.

He whistled as he walked down the sidewalk, the plastic-wrapped box tucked under one arm. He wanted her to have nice shoes because he wanted her to keep running. Those early morning runs had started to become the best part of his day. He'd been totally wrong when he'd thought he knew everything about Jessie. Sure, when she talked about her life she often kept the filter off, but he was learning things about her that he'd never known in all their years of friendship. Like the fact that she spent her nights watching cooking shows and home shopping channels, or that she worried about how much she talked to Prince Travis. Just a few days earlier, she'd told him that in the years her parents were away, she'd consoled herself by imagining them to be doing something exciting. "It was my fantasy that they were living double lives as spies," she explained. "I would watch spy movies with Wren, and we agreed that my parents were probably zipping around Europe in some sexy car, shooting at bad guys." She'd grown quiet. "It seems stupid, but it sounded better than selling computer components." He'd never wanted to hug her as badly as he had right at that moment.

They hadn't talked about the kiss since it happened almost a week ago, but then, they hadn't talked about Quinn, either. The more time that passed, the more the entire incident felt like something he might have imagined, or some misunderstanding. Nate hated that it was unresolved, but he didn't know how to fix it, and he didn't want to address it until he felt better prepared. Ultimately, he was glad that Jessie was on board with the road race, which Tom was calling the "Sweet Relief 5K." She was going to run, and she was going to create solid chocolate finisher's medals. It would be the perfect way for her to promote her new business venture.

As for his business...he was back at the drawing board. There were simply no spaces in the surrounding towns that would be appropriate for a gym, and if Mr.

Dinardo wasn't going to budge on the price, Nate didn't have a lot of options.

He pulled open the door to Hedda's, stepping in as the bell above the door chimed. Jessie was standing beside a table in the corner, taking orders. She didn't see him, so he crossed behind her to the counter, where Emily was measuring coffee. "Hey, Emily."

She was a pretty girl with a nice smile and clear, green eyes. He only knew her casually, but from what Jessie said, she was considering med school. She was focused, too, because she looked up and smiled warmly without a break in her task. "Good morning, Nate. You're here to see Jessie, I presume."

"I brought something for her." He lifted the bag and set it on the counter.

"I'm sure she'll be right over. Looks like she's finishing up."

He glanced over his shoulder at Jessie and felt that familiar longing in his chest. She had her blonde hair pulled back in a ponytail that curled up at the end, and she was wearing a pink T-shirt, white chinos, and a black apron. As she stood there, she scratched at her ankle with the toe of her opposite shoe. Adorable. Hell, they were running together three days a week at four in the morning, and he could say with certainty that she looked pretty cute right out of bed, though she'd never believe him if he told her that.

Emily looked up at him from beneath her lashes. "Can I get you anything while you wait? I'm brewing some fresh coffee."

"Nah. I can't stay long, but thanks."

He was heading out to the country club in a few minutes. Man, there was a topic for avoidance. Jessie hadn't mentioned joining him for lunch there again, but he knew that something like that would only lead to trouble. What could she possibly want with a stuffy lunch with stuffy people? She wasn't like that, which was exactly what made her great.

She turned away from the table and tucked the pencil in her hand behind her ear. When she saw him, her face brightened. "Didn't I just see you?"

He held out the bag. "I have something for you."

"For me?" She couldn't disguise the excitement in her voice as she reached eagerly for her gift. "You didn't have to do that!" She set the bag on the counter and nearly tore into it.

"If you're going to be training for a road race, you can't wear those sneakers you've been wearing. You need these, trust me. Your entire body will thank me."

He paused. Entire body? That wasn't what he'd — that had come out sort of...well. At least Jessie hadn't noticed. Her jaw dropped and her blue eyes widened as she pulled the running shoes out of the box. Her bright pink running shoes. "Wow, Nate! These are beautiful!" She paused, then set them back in the box. "I can't accept this, though. It's too much money."

Damn it. That wasn't the reaction he'd been hoping for. He pushed them toward her, gently. "It's a late birthday gift."

"No it isn't. You gave me that beer T-shirt for my birthday."

Yeah, he had. It wasn't his finest moment, and a psychologist would probably tell him it was evidence of stunted emotions or something. "That's a collector's item, I'll have you know. And that was before I knew you'd be running a 5K. Now I want to give you this."

Just accept them, he thought. He needed her to accept them. Was it so wrong that he wanted to do something nice for her? But he saw her turning it over in her mind, wondering what the catch was and to what extent she was going to be in his debt. He swept his hand down his face, feeling exasperated at how complicated everything was when all he wanted to do was to give her a pair of shoes. "No strings attached. I know the owner, and he gave me a discount. You need running shoes."

"I'd listen to your personal trainer," Emily said with a small smile. "He seems to know what he's talking about."

Nate waved an arm in Emily's direction. "See? Emily knows."

Jessie was staring down at the box, but she slowly brought her eyes upward to meet his gaze, a smile spreading across her beautiful lips. If only she had any idea how she could devastate him with that smile. "All right," she said. "Thank you. That was very thoughtful. But you should know that I'm going to repay you."

Here we go. "You don't have to. It's a gift."

"No, I've been thinking a lot about...things," she continued as she turned the shoes on their side and slid them back into the box. "I was thinking that I'd like to set you up with someone."

He glanced over his shoulder and then back again at her. "You're talking to me?"

"Yes, you," she laughed. "I've been thinking about myself too much, and I don't like that. You've been a good friend, and I'd like to do something nice for you. So I'm going to set you up with one of my friends."

Nate took a deep breath and told himself not to snap. Her heart was kind of in the right place, right? But did she think that he wasn't capable of getting dates of his own? And he was starting to get damn sick of this song and dance between them — the one where he went out of his way to show Jessie what he thought of her, and then she went ahead and missed the clue entirely. His stomach tightened. It was long past time for him to take the hint and realize she wasn't interested.

He pushed away from the counter and pulled himself up to his full height. Then he attempted a smile that felt downright painful. "I don't need you to set me up with anyone."

She blinked her large eyes and drew closer. "I have the perfect person in mind. She's an old friend of mine, and her name is Heather MacKenzie."

"Heather?" He nearly groaned.

Jessie halted. "You know her?"

Sure, he knew her, and he knew her well enough to know that he wasn't interested. She grew up on the cliffs, and she was the girl in high school who sneered at people like him. And Jessie. "You're actually friendly with her?"

He didn't really have to ask. Of course they were friends. Jessie was friends with everyone. She looked flustered for a moment, so he continued on. "It's a nice thought, but I'm not interested."

"If you gave her a chance —"

His neck started to heat. He'd come in there to give the girl he was actually in love with a thoughtful gift, because he was a fool and he still held out hope that she'd stop chasing a guy who wasn't interested and see the one who was. And her response was to fix him up with someone else.

He was finished.

"You want me to date someone?" Nate turned to the girl behind the counter, who was trying to look like she wasn't eavesdropping. "Hey, Emily? Are you seeing anyone these days?"

Emily looked up, stunned. "I'm not — no."

Beside him, Jessie's gaze was darting back and forth between him and Emily. "Well, wait. What about Heather?"

"Forget Heather," he said. "Emily, are you busy on Friday? Would you like to grab dinner?"

Even as he asked, he knew it was all wrong. He was only half watching as Emily's face lit up and she eagerly smiled. The person whose reaction he was waiting for was Jessie. She was shifting from left to right and fidgeting with her apron, probably coming up with some kind of reason he and Emily shouldn't go out together. The petty part of his brain thought, *Bingo*.

"I'd love to." Emily beamed. "Hold on a sec. I'll give you my number."

"Great."

Nate waited while Emily headed back toward the kitchen. He glanced over at Jessie, who was looking slightly shell-shocked. "Is that okay with you?" he said. "You're always talking about how nice Emily is, so I just thought —"

"No. I mean, yes, she's really nice." Jessie swallowed and looked down at her apron. "I should get back to work. Thanks for the shoes."

"We're running on Thursday morning, right?"

"Yes, that sounds good." She slid the bag off the counter and pressed it against her chest, over her heart. "Thanks again for the shoes."

"You're welcome."

She headed for the kitchen just as Emily was coming out. The two didn't look at each other as they crossed paths. "Here's my number," Emily said to him, holding out a slip of yellow notebook paper. "I included my email, too. Just in case."

He folded the paper without looking at it and put it in his pocket. "I'll give you a call later."

"Or you can text me."

She was grinning, and Nate felt a stab of guilt. Then he told himself there was nothing to feel bad about. He and Emily could go out and hit it off. Maybe he'd forget all about Jessie, and finally move on. He nodded. "Or I'll text you. Stay tuned."

It could have been his lucky day.

He had a date with Emily, and he had so many people signed up for yoga that he had to create a waiting list. It was either that or violate the fire code by overfilling the room. His friend Jim was thrilled. He was the Director of Member Activities, a title that, as he explained it, made him a "glorified scheduler."

"I hire people to run recreational programs, then I fill in their names on this dry-erase board with different colored markers," Jim explained as he flourished a blue marker. "Like so: Yoga Burn with Nate." He wrote the words and capped the marker with a mock-satisfied grin on his face. "Now it's official."

"What the hell is Yoga Burn?" Nate scratched at his neck. "I'm only doing sun salutations and some downward dogs."

"Throw in a few warrior poses and a triangle pose here or there," Jim said, tossing the marker to the side of a desk that was overflowing with papers. "The 'burn' is what gives your class a waiting list. It's all about marketing."

Jim set his hands on his hips. They'd known each other for years and had run track together in high school. Jim had placed second in states in the shot put. Since then he'd gotten a little thicker around the middle, and his white polo shirt pulled across a round stomach. "You should've been in marketing," Nate said.

"That's the plan, actually." Jim rounded his desk and sat on the edge, in the only clear space. "I've been working with a head hunter. I need a change. Ever since the divorce..." He shook his head. "I've always lived in Archer Cove. It's time to get out."

Nate had never seriously considered living anywhere else, but he thought he understood the need for a change. "Good luck with that."

"Thanks. In the meantime" — Jim folded his arms across his chest — "you should think about options."

He studied his friend, but Jim wasn't giving anything up. "What options?"

"I've had a second interview with a place in New York. Not the city, a little outside. I should hear back this week, and if so, I'm going to need to find a replacement. I think you'd be perfect."

Nate's first response was to laugh. "As a recreational manager at a country club?" Everything about the idea seemed horrible.

"No, as the *Director of Member Activities*," Jim said. "They'd hire you like that," he said with a snap of his fingers. "It's not a bad job. I've been here for almost eight years. The salary is decent, and so are the benefits. Most of the members are pretty cool, though you have the occasional pain in the ass who thinks we should offer things like polo. And yeah, they mean the kind with the horse."

Nate winced. "Yeah, it sounds great. Where can I sign up?"

"All joking aside, it's a decent job that lets you make a lot of connections. I got that interview in New York because of one of the members." He eyed Nate, slightly tilting his head to the side. "I'm trying to help you out. What are you doing now, running from rich person's house to rich person's house, showing them how to do bicep curls? This is a chance for you to get in somewhere. Get some stability and health insurance."

Jim's gaze was steady, the scrutiny uncomfortable. Nate stuffed his hands into his pockets and couldn't help but wonder why all of his friends seemed to think he needed help getting his life in order. "I like what I do," he said. "I help people, and if I worked here, where would my clients go?"

"They'd go *here*, buddy." Jim pushed off of the desk. "We have a full recreational facility. That means weight room, cardio room, and pool. You can talk to management about offering personal training. They're open to new ideas. *Plus*, and this is the best part, you'd get a referral fee for every new member you bring in. Let me tell you, those fees add up quickly. Then if you can convince your rich clients to also pay you for personal training sessions..." Jim whistled and shook his head. "Let's just say you'd be doing well for yourself."

He turned that over in his mind. It was true that to an extent, his income was capped as it was. There were only so many clients he could accommodate in a day. But Nate was fine with what he earned, even if it wasn't all that impressive. It was nowhere near what Quinn earned, for example. He took a deep breath.

He was earning a living as a freelancer, and where was that getting him, anyway? The girl of his dreams was treating him like he didn't even exist because she was hung up on the guy who earned the impressive salary.

He rubbed at the back of his neck. "I don't know, Jim. I guess I'll think about it."

"That's all I'm asking. Hey, you're on the way to yoga, right? You want a bottled water?" Without waiting for the answer, he walked over to a small refrigerator in the corner of the office and removed two bottles.

"Thanks, I'm all set."

Jim shrugged and tapped the door closed with his foot. "If you change your mind, you can help yourself." He twisted the top off his own bottle and grinned. "Your class is sold out, and that's never happened. People here like you. It's nice to be appreciated."

The comment struck Nate as a perfect summary of his life. It was nice to be appreciated, all right. At least his clients appreciated him, and maybe they'd follow, and maybe he could help more people if he took the job. "Thanks for thinking of me," he said. "I'm definitely interested."

CHAPTER TEN

JESSIE STIRRED THE thick, buttery batter with the red rubber spatula. Her hands were covered in flour, as was her apron. On the counter before her was a chaotic spread: paper butter wrappers and eggshells, spilled sugar crystals, and smears of flour. She only baked messy when she felt messy.

Jessie had never actually seen auras before, though she'd always been jealous of those who claimed to have that ability. But on the day that Emily made plans to go out with Nate, she felt as though she could actually *feel* her own aura, and it felt spiky and irritable. Before the day was done, someone might lose an eye.

Not that this was Emily's fault. She'd done nothing wrong, and so Jessie felt bad for avoiding her. It was just that if she looked her in the eyes, she felt certain that Emily would be able to tell how much it bothered her that she was going out with Nate. She was even more afraid that Emily would know why she was bothered, and even Jessie couldn't figure that part out. So she hid herself in the kitchen and directed an unusual amount of attention to baking scones and mulling over her feelings. She sure had a lot of them right then, and the ugliest was the painful jealousy that ricocheted inside her chest like she was a human pinball machine.

I am a chocolate warrior. I am focused on my goal in a single-minded, obsessive way that is totally healthy and functional. That day, the affirmations were coming out all wrong.

She dropped cups of wild blueberries into the batter and slowed her aggressive stirring, blending them carefully. Yes, she was jealous. She could admit that. After all, Nate was a dear friend, and she was used to having him around. It was only natural that she'd fear being supplanted by Emily. Except she knew that wasn't the problem, exactly. She wasn't afraid to lose pizza-and-beer nights with Nate — not when all she could think about was that single, perfect kiss, and about how he might go and kiss Emily that way, too.

She set the spatula down beside the bowl, feeling ill.

"You okay?" Uncle Hank asked from the small desk at the back of the kitchen. He peered at her from above a stack of documents. "You look pale."

"I'm fine, thanks." Jessie inhaled and reached for the spatula. "Just thinking, that's all."

"If it's anything you want to talk about, I'm here."

She smiled. "Thanks." She most certainly would not be discussing any of this with her uncle.

Jessie lifted the batter from the metal mixing bowl and set it on the floured surface, smoothing it into a

169

circle. She sliced the dough into triangles, set them on a baking sheet, and sprinkled the tops with sugar. As she was opening the door to the industrial stainless-steel oven, Emily walked into the kitchen. No, make that bounced.

"I just locked up. Should I run to the bank?" She held up a navy blue deposit bag.

Jessie slipped the baking sheet onto the oven rack and closed the door. "I could do it on my way out."

"You're busy," said Uncle Hank. "I'll head over. I could use a walk." He stood and stretched behind the desk before approaching Emily, arm outstretched. "Good day?"

"Very. Jessie, I sold a few boxes of your chocolates."

Jessie couldn't meet her smile, so she looked down at the floor instead. "That's great." She crouched down to the black-and-white checkered tile floor and pretended to pick something up. "I should sweep the floors."

"I can do that," Emily chirped, reaching for the broom.

Jessie's shoulders tightened and rose closer to her ears. Did Emily have to take *everything*? She ground her teeth and headed back to her messy workspace on the counter. As she collected the broken eggshells and the butter wrappers and dropped them into the trash, Emily pushed the broom merrily across the floor. Jessie half expected her to break into song and swing on the hanging pot rack like she was trapped in some damn musical. People shouldn't be that chipper in real life.

Emily glanced up from her happy sweeping. "Did you end up applying for that small business loan? It seemed like you were interested in it, but I haven't heard anything else."

"I'm working on it." Jessie's forehead was tight. "It's going to take me a while. I've got to put together a marketing plan, form a company. There's no rush, since there's nowhere in town to put a chocolate shop."

The thought stirred something small and self-pitying inside of her. She felt herself getting into a bad spot and she needed something — or someone — to pull her out of her doldrums. Who could she turn to? Let's see: Quinn had dumped her, and Nate had put her in a foul mood. Jessie crushed an eggshell in her hands before tossing it into the trash.

"Something will come along," Emily said. She stooped to lift a dustpan from the floor and empty it into the trash. "I'm excited about my date. Nate texted me. We're going to Sam's." She paused. "I hope you don't mind."

Jessie started. "Yes. I mean, no, of course not. Why would I mind? I don't mind."

Emily leaned against the propped handle of the broom. "I just know you and Nate are friends, and you and I work together. I want to make sure nothing's strange." She smiled and resumed sweeping. "I was thinking it would be a lot of fun if we went on a double date. Oh!" She froze, her eyes wide. "You and Quinn...I forgot. I didn't mean —"

"It's okay," Jessie said abruptly, needing a change of subject. "Don't even worry about it."

"Sometimes I say the stupidest things," Emily muttered, more to herself. She continued to sweep, but moved quickly away to the other side of the kitchen.

Jessie felt a twist of guilt. Emily was one of her friends, and so was Nate, and it was great that two nice people were going out together. She set the spatula in the metal bowl, carried them both to the sink, and turned on the hot water. "It was a nice thought, Em. And you really shouldn't feel bad. Quinn and I are only taking a break." It sounded less and less convincing every time she said it.

She scrubbed the pots, pans, bowls, and utensils that were piled in and around the sink, dried them, and then wiped down the counters. By then, the scones were finished. Jessie was just setting them on a tray when her cell phone rang. When she saw the number, her mood instantly lifted. "Wren! How are you?"

"Low on chocolate stock," her cousin said. "We had a large tasting party last night and we paired wine and chocolate. Do you think you can swing by? I can send you an order sheet."

Jessie was proud to be the exclusive supplier of chocolate at Wren and Jax's Cliffside Vineyards, and Wren was exactly the person who could lift Jessie's mood. Selfishly, she couldn't have been happier that her cousin was running low on inventory. "I can load your order right now and come right over. Just tell me what you need."

The catering van was white and roomy, and the words "Hedda's Bakery — Catering" were painted on one side in purple. In the back were rows of racks to secure trays of food. Uncle Hank had purchased the van used when a local restaurant was looking to unload it. Jessie had taken advantage, offering catering as a means to raise a little extra money for Hedda's. At one point, her Auntie Lil had even helped her with the menu. But business over the past year had slowed down as more competition crept into the area, so Jessie had devoted more attention to her chocolates. The van was convenient, though. They still had a few catering jobs a month, and it was perfect for carrying large orders of chocolate.

Wren and Jax were her best customers, which wasn't saying all that much. She'd stop by every other week with an order, and they always paid her and gave her a few bottles of wine from the vineyard as a tip. As Jessie wound the van up the hills to Cliffside Vineyards, she hoped they'd spare a bottle of ice wine. She loved the sweet, syrupy treat, and she and Nate had whiled away quite a few evenings in the cottage sipping small glasses.

Jessie's heart pivoted in place. It was like she kept forgetting about how complicated things with Nate had suddenly become. Maybe he and Emily would really hit it off, and then it wasn't like they'd be drinking ice wine together very often anymore. Not alone, with him teasing her about the silly things that secretly made her cry, and her teasing him about his weirdo workout routine ideas, like that time he was going to make a client do pull-ups

173

on monkey bars. This was what she'd lose if Emily was in the picture.

Jessie bit the inside of her cheek. It was just one date, not marriage. No need to get ahead of herself.

The vineyard itself was easy to miss, set back as it was from a narrow, rarely traveled road that jutted through a dense forest of pine. A carved wooden sign announced "Cliffside Vineyards" in simple type. It was only when one followed the long gravel drive that one saw the hidden gem: acres of rolling vineyards overlooking a sliver of the ocean; a newly constructed red barn that included a comfortable tasting room with a long bar, an imposing stone fireplace, and a large deck for summertime gatherings; and a renovated white farmhouse with a wraparound porch that was exceedingly modest by Hollywood standards, but was the place Wren and Jax called home. It was the sort of property that few found by accident, but if they did, they were rewarded with a spectacular experience.

When she arrived, the tasting room was closing for the evening and the visitors' parking lot was empty. She continued up the hill to the farmhouse. As she drew closer, she saw that the lights were on. Jessie could smell marinara sauce. She pulled a shipping box filled with truffles out of the van and lugged it to the front porch. Fortunately, Jax opened the door before Jessie was forced to decide how she was going to ring the doorbell. "I thought I was going to have to shout at you to get off my property," he joked, and lifted the box from her arms. "What is this, more chocolate?"

174

"Wren called in an order. She said you had a tasting."

His strong arms handled the box easily. "She's in charge of that. Did you eat? We're just sitting down and we have plenty."

"It smells great." She reached up to give him a kiss on the cheek. "You had a nice time in France?"

He wrinkled his handsome face and gave a noncommittal shrug. "I didn't get to see much of it. All your cousin ever wants to do is have sex with me. Ow!" He winced as Wren came up from behind and whacked him in the shoulder. "It's true."

Jessie had heard all about Jax long before she'd actually met him. Who hadn't? He'd been all over the celebrity gossip blogs, always with a different woman. The best, most surprising thing about Jax was that beneath the brash exterior, he was a softie who loved to spend his evenings chatting in the kitchen at Hedda's and helping the family to bake. What Jessie loved most about him was seeing the look on his face every time Wren was around. He was like a lost puppy when she entered the room.

But as Jax was looking at Wren with his characteristic adoration, Wren was rolling her eyes in mock consternation. "Those are for the event we have on Friday night. I'm putting everything in the hall."

"Yes, ma'am." He winked at Jessie before turning and heading into the home.

Wren reached for Jessie's hand. "Come in. We're just having dinner. I'll get you a plate."

The smells of pasta, marinara sauce, and garlic sent Jessie's stomach rumbling — she hadn't eaten anything since breakfast. Her gaze took in the domestic scene: the farmhouse, with its wide floorboards and light yellow walls, and Wren and Jax in blue jeans, light sweaters, and socks, joking and smiling at each other. The thought of returning to her empty cottage made her heart sink.

She said eagerly, "I'd love to."

Jessie envied the chef's kitchen, with its stainless-steel appliances, generous granite countertops, and wide picture window overlooking the stretch of vineyards. It had been designed for their gourmet chef, Tyrone, who lived in the guest quarters whenever Jax was preparing for a movie and needed to be in peak physical shape. As far as Jessie knew, Wren was trying to pick up some cooking basics, but she'd always been a sandwich and frozen pizza kind of girl. As she pulled up a stool at the breakfast bar at the center island, Jessie was secretly thrilled that Tyrone was back in LA. When he was around, dinners were vegetable-based with small portions of lean meats and unsweetened berries for dessert. He *never* would have cooked this dinner, which looked and smelled amazing.

She inhaled as Jax spooned a serving of bowtie pasta and sauce into a white bowl and set it before her. Wren said, "It's nothing fancy, but we made the sauce ourselves from the Roma tomatoes that grew in our garden last summer."

"Nothing fancy?" Jessie said. "I was just thinking that if I could, I'd unhinge my jaw and devour this entire bowl all at once."

"Now there's a visual," Jax said pleasantly, and set a bowl in front of Wren. "Do you want water, darling?"

"Darling." Jessie giggled. "You two are so gross."

"I'd love one," Wren said, and shot Jessie a knowing look. "Like Quinn has never used a pet name for you?"

Jessie picked up her fork and stabbed at her pasta. "Nope. And we broke up." She took a bite. Wow. Worth the calories.

In her peripheral vision, she saw Wren's eyes widen with concern. "You did? You didn't tell me this."

"It's not important. We're taking a little break so he can focus on his career. No big deal."

"A break? What's that mean?" Wren's pretty face was scrunched, as if she'd just caught a whiff of something that stunk.

"He's working so many hours these days that it's hard for him to focus on a relationship." She poked a piece of pasta too aggressively, and it flew over the side of her bowl. "This sauce is great, by the way. You should consider canning it. You could put your pretty faces on the label."

Jax was bustling around the kitchen, opening cabinets and slicing lemons and trying — so it seemed to Jessie — to appear that he wasn't listening. "Jess? Lemon or lime?"

"Lemon, please. Anyway, as far as Quinn goes," she said around a mouthful, "it's okay with me. I am *also* focusing on my career. I'm going to open my own shop, really work on selling my chocolates. I figure I've been developing my line for so long, I should go all in. What am I waiting for, right?"

"Well, I think *that* is great news. You work so hard that I can't imagine that you wouldn't be a household name. If there's anything we can ever do to help...I'd love to invest in you."

Jessie warmed at the offer, but she could never ask her cousin to put money into her business. "That's so sweet. But I'm going to be applying for a loan. It's a lot of paperwork, and it's a little intimidating, to be honest, but I was thinking it's time to suck it up and figure out how to make some graphs to demonstrate projected growth. But thanks anyway. I'll let you know."

"Absolutely." Wren paused and looked down at her plate as if she was trying to decide what to say next. Then she picked up her fork and held it in midair. "His career, huh? That's the excuse he gave you?"

Jessie mulled this one over as she chewed. Jax set a glass of ice water in front of her and said, "This sounds like it's going in a particular direction, and there's a game on —"

"Go ahead," Wren said, lifting her glass. "Everyone without a vagina is excused."

"Thank God," he muttered. "I'll be back in a bit to clean up."

Jessie watched him walk out before leaning closer to Wren and whispering, "You have *Jax Cosgrove* doing dishes? What kind of kink did that take?"

Wren gave her a wry grin. "I'm lucky that here in this house, we both forget that he's some Hollywood hotshot. But don't change the subject. Look, I'm enjoying my bowtie noodles, but when you tell me that Quinn dumped you to focus on his career, I smell pasta and bullshit."

"I don't want to talk about Quinn." And she didn't. Her stomach had started to knot as she thought about the real reason she'd been so relieved her cousin had called and given her an excuse to visit. She tried to sound upbeat. "You know, Emily and Nate are going out. On Friday. It's just a first date, so who knows. It could be serious."

When Wren didn't answer, Jessie dragged a bowtie around the bottom of her bowl, making little wave patterns in the sauce. Then as the silence dragged on, she did what she seemed to do best those days: turn off her brain and plow ahead. "And I'm happy for them. Who wouldn't be, when they're both such nice people. Nice people should end up together. Like you and Jax. You're both nice, too." Jessie took a breath. "I was going to set him up with Heather MacKenzie. I thought they'd hit it off, because Nate is all into physical fitness, and Heather...you know."

"Heather? Seriously?" Wren shook her head vehemently. "I would never see them together. And isn't she dating that politician? A state senator or something?"

"Oh yeah? I guess we've lost touch."

There was another stretch of silence. Then Wren started chuckling. "You were really going to set him up with Heather MacKenzie? Why would you do that? Nate's such a great guy!"

At first Jessie opened her mouth to defend herself, but Wren kept on laughing, and really, what defense did

Jessie have, when she'd essentially decided to set up two single friends because they were...well, single. She started to giggle. "Come on, Heather is nice enough."

"If you like piranhas in Gucci. Nate is much too down-to-earth for her. Emily may be a better match." She took a sip of her water and then said, "You're funny. Your heart is where it should be, and I love you for that, but sometimes your schemes are so...elaborate. You're always looking for the complicated solution. Like Nate and Heather. Nate and Emily are a great match, and right in front of you." She shook her head. "And like your chocolates. I'll write you a check tonight and let you skip the whole business loan thing if you allow me to. It's my money, from my latest project."

"Ooh, latest project? You didn't tell me about that."

"It's a vampire romance."

Jessie wrinkled her nose and giggled again. "Vampire romance? That sounds awful."

"It's not that bad," Wren laughed. "And again with changing the subject! You're hard to pin down tonight!"

Jessie lifted another forkful of pasta and smiled, feeling suddenly lighter than she'd felt all day, even though nothing had been resolved. Friends could do that, make you feel like all the troubles in your life were a little bit funnier than you'd realized. "I haven't told you my biggest news yet," she said. "I'm running a 5K."

Wren nearly choked on her pasta. She clapped her linen napkin across her mouth and laughed silently. When she finally managed to collect herself, tears were forming at the corners of her eyes. "How in the world did you not mention this sooner? Okay, please tell me you have a camera crew documenting your every footstep, because that's television gold right there."

Jessie filled Wren in on the details, but kept a few out. Like the fact that she'd started running in order to fit in her maid of honor dress. Or the fact that she had an odd case of butterflies in her stomach at the thought of seeing Nate first thing in the morning in his sexy running shorts. Sure, sometimes Jessie shared too much, but every now and then, she had enough sense to know which things were better left unsaid.

"I sort of enjoy running," she confessed. "Emphasis on *sort of*, and I think it's mostly because of the company." Jessie caught a fleeting arch to Wren's eyebrows, and her cheeks grew hot. "With Nate. I mean, he's funny. He makes me, um, not think about running."

She may as well have been naked just then, she felt so exposed. But Wren had the good grace to simply reach over, stroke the ends of Jessie's hair, and say, "You're worthy of love. You know that, right? You're worthy of someone who stares at you like you're a goddess and doesn't put you second to his career. Maybe you already know someone like that?"

Jessie's face was so hot that all she could do was stare at the napkin in her lap. "Maybe. I don't know."

"Uh huh." Wren stood up from her stool and stretched. "You're in a shame spiral, Jess. I've been there. The sooner you step back and say that you won't accept second place — and actually mean it — the sooner you'll find what you're looking for. I'm guessing it's staring you smack in the face."

Jessie swallowed the tightness in her throat, her heart still hammering away in her chest. Man, "shame spiral" didn't sound like something she wanted to be a part of, but that was exactly where she was, wasn't it? Ashamed of her looks, ashamed of *herself*. Why did she think she needed to change, anyway? Screw Quinn and his stupid country club manners.

She hated eating her cereal dry and her oatmeal plain. She hated feeling like she had to be someone else to make Quinn love her. Maybe she couldn't afford a fancy dress and frequent pedicures, but she had a little chocolate business that she'd started all on her own, and she was darn proud of that. Something shifted, and Jessie breathed easier. She felt okay. She should celebrate.

"You want some dessert?" Wren said as she pulled open the freezer and stuck her head in. "I've got fudge swirl ice cream, mint chocolate chip, and a flavor called crème brûlée." She glanced over her shoulder. "Choices are made for other things. I think we should have a little of each and call it a tasting."

Jessie grinned and stood to clear her plate. "It's like you read my mind."

CHAPTER ELEVEN

NATE HAD DOWNED three glasses of cold water before leaving his apartment, but his legs still felt like lead. He never should've let Quinn talk him into that beer and wings. Now he was going to be fighting dehydration all day. If he was lucky, he had another water bottle rolling around somewhere in the back. If he wasn't, well, he'd only be paying the Stupid Tax.

Quinn had called him after dinner the previous night. He and Caryn were fighting again. "It's her ex-boyfriend," he said, his fingers hooked around the neck of a beer bottle. "I know he's trying to get back together with her."

They were sitting in Desmond's out in Spencer, just a dive bar with loud music, sticky round wooden tables, and plenty of people looking to get laid. Nate had once found a line of cocaine in the men's bathroom, right there on the windowsill. Needless to say, it wasn't his favorite place, but it was where Quinn was drinking.

"Is that what she said, that her ex wants to get back together?" Nate stifled a yawn into his fist. It was only ten o'clock, but he'd been waking early to run with Jessie, and it was catching up with him.

"She didn't say it, but then I see her texting someone and when I ask her about it, she won't tell me who she's talking to." Quinn clenched his teeth. "I think she's hiding something."

Quinn had always had this type-A, control freak streak. Usually he managed to keep it in check or to channel his energy in more appropriate ways, like into work. Caryn seemed to bring out the worst sides of him. "If you're going to be in a relationship with her, you need to trust her. If that's a problem, then you shouldn't be in a relationship."

Quinn tilted the beer bottle against his lips, watching Nate the entire time. He let out a belch as he set the bottle back down on the table. "Me and Caryn have a dynamic. I wouldn't expect most people to understand it." The words came out like *unnerstan it*.

Nate thought he *unnerstood it* just fine. "Basically you're worried that Caryn's going to do to you what you did to Jessie. Isn't that it? Because in your mind, that's how people treat each other."

Even more than he hated the hostility in his voice, Nate hated the way his anger wound itself through his gut. Quinn had been his best friend for twenty-five years. He was part of himself. But Quinn was acting like a real asshole lately, and friends set each other straight.

"I didn't do anything to Jessie," Quinn said, lifting his finger to point at Nate across the table. "I did the honorable thing and broke up with her."

"Honorable my ass. Don't tell me that you weren't fooling around with Caryn before that night."

Quinn looked like he was going to argue, but then a slow smile spread across his lips. "It's hotter when it's wrong."

Nate wanted to throw the table across the room and have it out right then. Instead, he'd grabbed Quinn's bottle right out of his hand and stood up. "Hey!" Quinn said. "That's my —"

"You're finished." Nate threw a few bills on the bar and grabbed his friend by the upper arm. "Let's go. I'm driving you home." *Again.*

Quinn tried to jerk himself free of Nate's grip, but it was useless. "I wasn't done. Did you hear me? I said —"

"You're done, all right. When you start talking like cheating is hot, you're fucking done."

Nate yanked him out of his chair and pulled him across the floor. After a few steps, Quinn stopped fighting. "Man. You like Jessie," he slurred.

Nate's heart skipped. "She's a sweet girl. And she's not the type to get into casual dating."

"If you're so worried about her, then *you* should date her." Quinn stood by the SUV, rolling slightly in place as he put a hand on Nate's shoulder. "There. I'm giving you my blessing."

Nate clenched his jaw. "That's how much she meant to you, huh?" He lifted Quinn's heavy hand from his shoulder and allowed it to drop.

Quinn looked like he was about to answer, but then he fumbled for the car door. It wasn't like Nate had been posing a real question, anyway. He knew that to Quinn, Jessie was just a casual fling. He'd move on, like he had a hundred times before, and he'd brag about how easy it all was for him. But this time, Nate wouldn't listen. This time, Nate couldn't indulge the boasting and chest-thumping. Because it was Jessie, and she deserved better.

He'd driven Quinn home and left him on the front steps to his house. Then he'd headed home and tried to sleep. He might have managed to squeeze in a few hours before the alarm went off.

When he arrived at the cottage, Jessie was waiting on the sidewalk, touching her toes to stretch out her hamstrings. She righted herself when he pulled up, watching him. "'Morning," she said.

"'Morning." His eyes stung with fatigue, and he yawned into his arm. "Sorry."

"It's okay." Jessie folded her arms across her chest and stepped closer to him. "Are you all right? You look tired —"

"Fine."

"Nate." She set her hand lightly on his wrist. The contact sent his heart racing. "We can do this another time. Later this afternoon, even. Go get some sleep."

She looked tired herself, with those red-rimmed eyes. "I'm okay to run," Nate said. "Are you?"

A flicker of hesitation before she nodded and said, "Yes. Fine. I'm ready to push to the brink of death, but no further."

"Then let's go, but keep it easy."

Dawn seeped through the clouds, even at that hour. Before he and Jessie had started running together, Nate had never woken so early — not on purpose, at least. He was still finding the early alarm painful, but he enjoyed the stillness of the hour, the smell of salt air in the breeze. He glanced at her as they ran together. She was focused on the road ahead, her brows knit in concentration, her cheeks puffing with each quick breath. For the first time in all of their runs, she was avoiding him: his eyes, his company, his existence. He didn't know what he wanted from her anymore. He only knew that it wasn't this.

"I'm going to take you somewhere new," he said. When he saw her eyes widen, he said, "Just trust me on this one. I promise you'll come out alive."

After a couple weeks of running, her stamina was improving and so was her speed. They ran to the end of the neighborhood, which cut off suddenly into a copse of thin pines split down the middle by a narrow, sandy pathway. Jessie stopped short. "Are we going on that thing?"

Like he was asking her to travel by camelback. "It's a little off-road. Nothing you can't handle, I promise."

But she stayed back, her hands on her hips, her head cocked. "What, are we going into the woods to light a bonfire and do keg stands?" Bullshit meter on high.

"You know, it's not actually weird to run on a trail. Some people even seek these opportunities out."

He waited for her to fire back some smart reply, but instead she shrugged and grumbled, "I should've brought my bug spray."

"You're an outdoorsy kind of girl, Jess," Nate said as she brushed past him down the path. "That's why I love you."

Shit. He said that out loud. Did she notice? She was jogging down the path, ducking below some hanging fir branches to reach a clearing. Nate waited a moment, holding his breath. When it seemed like he'd possibly gotten away with it, he exhaled. That was close. Not that he couldn't have laughed it off, said it was just a figure of speech, but —

"That's a mean thing to say, Nate." Her voice was soft, barely audible above the sound of their breathing.

"What, are you saying that you're really outdoorsy?" He forced a laugh. "Come on, I'm teasing."

Beside him, she was quiet. "You know what I meant. I've had enough of people telling me they love me and not meaning it."

His throat constricted. He didn't dare try to follow up with an explanation. Or a confession.

The path broke through the trees and cut through a dense spread of vegetation: stretches of pink Carolina rose and bearberry that ended at a small sandy hill tufted with beach grass. When she reached the top of the hill, Jessie stopped again. There she stood.

"You've gotten faster," he said. "You didn't even take the walk breaks."

She stepped down the hill as if he weren't there at all. Nate followed with a sigh as they both arrived at a small sandy beach. Here, the waves lapped the shore softly, and thumbnail-sized pink seashells littered the beach, together with the occasional stray crab leg. "I used to come down here all the time when I was a kid," Nate explained. "It's a great place for catching crabs in a bucket. This one time, I found a tiny turtle —"

"Look at all of these seashells," Jessie whispered as she stooped to get a better look. "I could spend hours down here. I never knew about this beach."

"No one comes here," he said, feeling proud. "It's cut off from the town beaches, and it's too small for recreation."

Around them, insects creaked and stirred. A seagull circled lazily overhead. He'd brought her to this beautiful place, and Jessie wouldn't look at him. *I almost punched my best friend out last night,* he wanted to say. *I was about to feed him my fist for cheating on you. Because I'm not teasing when I say that I love you. I'm actually not being mean.*

"This seems like the kind of place where you're supposed to think deep thoughts, doesn't it? So, do you ever think about what you want from life?" Her voice sliced through the air. "I've been thinking about it a lot lately. Like, I want my own storefront, a pink polka-dotted awning, and maybe a thigh gap. Just a modest one. I think with those things, I'd be happy."

"A pink polka-dotted awning and a thigh gap is all it takes, huh?" He poked at a purple-freckled seashell with the toe of his right sneaker. "I guess I'd want similar things. Not the thigh gap, but to feel successful, professionally."

"What about personally?" Jessie was sitting in the sand, resting her chin on her knees as she gazed out over the water. "Do you think you'll settle down?"

"Yeah, I guess so. Maybe. If I find the One."

She turned her face to look at him. "How will you know she's the One?"

He considered the question. "She'll know when and where to use her teeth, and when we're done having sex, she won't start laughing."

"Ha!" Jessie beamed and lifted her head. "Spoken like a true romantic."

"You think I'm joking? I could tell you stories." But he was laughing, too, and for a moment, the tension between them slipped away.

He thought of his date with Emily. How childish and impulsive and *wrong* of him that was, when the only woman he could ever imagine himself with was sitting beside him already. Hell, she could break out in a fit of giggles after they had sex if she wanted, or bite him in all the wrong places. She'd still be the One.

He crouched beside her, allowing one knee to touch the sand. "Jess, I —"

"It's okay. Whatever it is. I can tell you're about to apologize to me for something, and don't worry about it."

She patted his knee, allowing their eyes to meet briefly. "You showed me this place. I forgive you."

She forgave him? For what?

Then in an instant, she was on her feet again. "We should head back. I've got another chocolate order coming, and I want to get in early."

Every inch of his body was weary and beaten down with fatigue. He rose to his feet with great effort, suddenly feeling a hundred years old. "Sure. Chocolate orders come first."

He did his best to make it sound light, but man. All he wanted was for her to slow down and spend a few minutes on him, and she was spending all of her attention on everything else. She was even jogging again, damn it. Following the path back into the woods, taking off without him. And for half an instant he wondered what she was so mad about, and then it hit him on the head. Emily, that was what.

He'd asked Emily out to piss her off, maybe even make her a little jealous. He didn't expect it to actually work.

"Hey, Jess?" Nate came up behind her and stayed at her elbow. "Emily and I are going out on Friday."

"I know," she said brightly. "I'm so happy for you two. Really. You'll have a great time. Emily's a nice girl."

Said without a trace of sarcasm. Was she mad at him or not? It was messing with his head. "I was wondering if you'd like to join us," he said. "Not like it would be the three of us. I'd invite Max."

She turned her head. "The SEAL?"

"Navy SEAL, yes. Not the animal."

Jessie fluttered her lips and slowed to a walk. They had reached the copse of trees again. The needles of a fir tree slipped softly across his arm. "I don't know about that," she said. "Max seems a little intense, and I think he undressed me with his eyes while he ate that chicken salad sandwich."

She was probably right, Nate thought. High-strung, intense Max was probably a terrible match for Jessie. That's what made the situation perfect. "You know, between you and me, I don't want Emily to get the wrong idea. I want to keep the first date casual, not move too quickly."

That got her attention. She stopped dead in her tracks. "So, wait. You want to double date because you want me to be a buffer between you and Emily?"

"'Buffer' is the wrong word. I just want to get to know her before we go out alone." He shrugged. "Maybe I'll hate her guts by the time appetizers roll around."

"I highly doubt that will happen."

Jessie looked at the pine trees around them as she stretched her neck. She was quiet for so long that he wondered if she'd lost her train of thought and had perhaps started contemplating string theory. Then she said, "I guess it's fine. It's not like I have anything else to do."

"I love your enthusiasm. I'll ask Max to refrain from visually assaulting you."

"That's fair. I'll tell Emily to lower her expectations. But it seems she already has." She tried not to laugh at her own joke, and failed.

God, did he love everything about her. "Hilarious, Jessica. If the chocolate thing doesn't work, you should do stand-up."

"I'm here all week, folks. Try the prime rib."

Nate rubbed his eyes and shook his head. "And still you keep going. Come on, I'll race you home."

Jessie clutched the manila folder to her chest as she stepped into the bakery kitchen. Uncle Hank was there first, as usual. He whistled and cracked an egg into a stainless-steel bowl. Jessie took inventory of the ingredients surrounding his workspace: flour, butter, sugar, milk, and blueberries. Her stomach began to growl. "Muffins or coffee cake?" she asked.

"Neither. I'm making a vanilla blueberry loaf cake with a sugar glaze. It's great with tea."

Jessie strolled around the counter to stand beside him. She snuck a few blueberries out of the bowl and said, "Uncle Hank, this is my business loan application. I made it with my hands." The folder made a slapping noise as it struck the counter. "I was up all night documenting my personal financial history and making bar graphs. I used teal, magenta, and canary yellow for the bars." She opened the folder to the appropriate page to show him. "See, the teal is year one of sales, magenta is year two, and canary yellow is projected growth over the next twelve months. It's sort of aspirational, but I did an Internet search and I think it works."

"It's definitely aesthetically pleasing," Uncle Hank said.

"I thought so. You know, loan officers live such dull lives, looking at numbers all day, thinking about creditworthiness. I thought, they need a bar graph with some magenta, and they just don't know it yet." She popped a blueberry into her mouth. "Mmm. These are good."

"I'm proud of you, honey. It's not easy to put yourself out there like this. Whatever happens with the loan, you've succeeded."

Jessie shut the folder and pushed it out of the way. Uncle Hank was unwrapping sticks of butter and dropping them into the bowl, and she didn't want her hard work to get greasy. "Thank you. I had dinner with Wren last night, and she got me thinking that I need to do this, not just talk about doing it."

Opening her own chocolate shop, that is. She needed to do it for herself, not to impress Quinn. Sweets were her passion, and even if her life was messy and imperfect, at least it could be passionate.

She was waiting by the door when the First Bank of Spencer opened at nine o'clock, and she marched right in and up to Fred White. He was coming from a back room, carrying a cup of coffee in a plain white mug. He probably liked beige. "Mr. White! Here's my application for a small business loan. I hope you find it up to your standards."

He accepted the proffered file with a furrowed brow. "Thank you, Jessie. You could have emailed everything to me."

Ah. She laughed nervously. "I was in the neighborhood. Just wanted to make sure it reached you safely. My email's been down. Hackers." The excuses came rapid fire.

"That's fine. Maybe next time." He blew steam over the brim of his mug and took a tentative sip. "I look forward to reviewing it."

"And I look forward to your judgment," she said. Then, after a few painful seconds of silence, Jessie realized that she couldn't possibly help her case if she continued on in that vein. "I'll see you later. I put my phone number on the application."

"Perfect. I'll bet it's right where it's supposed to be. Have a good day." He ducked into his office and set his mug on his naked desk. Then he shut his door in her face.

Jessie swept her palms down her shirt and felt like mostly, she'd accomplished something great. She'd filed an application for a loan, and she'd exercised her business sense with Mr. White and not screwed anything up too badly. As she stepped outside and into the sunshine, a bolt of sparks burst in her stomach. Until that moment, with the application still un-filed, she hadn't allowed the thought to register: she was going on a sort-of date with Nate. As a buffer between him and Emily, but still. She was kind of his wingman, a position of honor and trust in the male kingdom. Maybe that was a good thing? Did guys kiss their wingmen?

She shook her head. No need to go there. It was a night out, that was all. But he wasn't serious about Emily. The window was open.

She hummed to herself as she strolled back to work. *I am the one who knocks on the chocolate door.* And things were starting to turn around for her.

CHAPTER TWELVE

SAM'S AFTER DARK was set on the rooftop, under the stars and a crisscross of white lights. Jessie and Wren had gone there on occasion, usually when there was something to celebrate. That night, the specials were gazpacho prepared with watermelon, and spicy fish tacos garnished with mango salsa and fresh guacamole. Jessie had decided in advance of the date that she was suspending her diet for the evening. She ordered both.

She'd also curled her hair. It felt a little bit like trying too hard, but she didn't give a damn. She'd also splurged on a new black top with a wide neck that exposed more of her shoulders, a pair of dark jeans, and black heels. Jessie was running late, and so Emily, Nate, and Max were already seated when she came running in. "Sorry!" she gushed. "My car — I accidentally turned on the radio and had to ask a neighbor to jump the engine."

"No problem at all." Max rose to his feet, his eyes wide as he looked her over. "You're worth waiting for, Jessie."

The compliment embarrassed her, and she looked to Nate. But he didn't speak. He was watching her, his lips slightly parted. Looking, she realized, like a lost puppy.

Her heart stalled. For the first time in as long as she could remember, Jessie felt gorgeous.

Of course Emily looked beautiful, too. Her light brown hair was pulled into one of those romantic braids, and she was wearing a white dress with cap sleeves that was really very sweet and pretty. But Nate wasn't looking at Emily, no matter how much she touched his arm or tried to engage him in conversation. He would answer her questions, or ask politely about her interests, but then he'd turn back to Jessie, who was sitting across the table from him. Jessie's heart was pounding in her throat so strongly that it was a wonder she could breathe at all.

"I did a fifteen-miler today," Max announced. "Lost another toenail."

"Oh, really?" Jessie lifted her drink to her lips.

She'd opted for a sangria mocktail, thinking she'd save enough calories that she'd be able to indulge in the bread basket. This, she quickly realized, had been a big mistake. She made a note to herself: where a blind date is involved, choose alcohol over bread.

"It doesn't actually hurt," Max explained, obviously mistaking the wrinkle in her nose for concern rather than repulsion. "It just turns black and falls off. I've thought of

198

having mine surgically removed. You know, for when I go racing."

"Racing?"

Jessie pressed her lips back together, but it was too late. The question was out, and Max was eager to answer.

"I'm what you'd call an extreme athlete," he explained. "I've completed a few double triathlons. That's a 4.8 mile swim, a 224-mile bike ride, and a 52.4-mile run. I usually place in my age group."

Was it her imagination, or had he flexed his biceps while telling her about that? Jessie reached for a bread roll and cursed the poor choices she'd made. "That sounds time-consuming," she said.

This was not the right response. Max lifted his chin and issued something that sounded like a snort. "Time-consuming? Let me put it this way: we all get only so many hours on this planet, and instead of rotting in front of the television, I choose to spend my time taking care of the only body I'm going to get."

"Mmmhmm." Jessie broke off a piece of bread and buttered it. "I didn't mean anything by it. But I'm actually one of those who likes television. I even like commercials."

Nate leaned forward, his forearms on the table. "Animal shelter commercials make her cry."

"They do," she said. "Also, I like home shopping. I watched this one segment with a set of knives that could slice up a turkey in less than two minutes. Literally. They had the timer going at the bottom of the screen and everything." She was getting excited just thinking about it.

"Anyway, I was broke at the time. Well, I'm always broke. But I was especially broke then, and so I didn't order the knives."

Emily, who had been listening politely, said, "So what happened?"

"That's it." Jessie shrugged. "I didn't order the knives, but now I watch that channel all the time and hope they'll come back on. I would carve turkeys every day of the week. Every day would be Thanksgiving. Em, wouldn't that be great? I was thinking I'd get a set for Hedda's."

"That's a great idea, actually," she said.

"I'm going to make a note to research those knives." Jessie reached for her mocktail and took another sip.

Max had grown uncomfortably silent. Also, he was staring at her in a way that made her check her shirt for stains. Nope, all clean there. "You watch home shopping," he said flatly.

"Totally. But if I have my choice, I prefer cooking shows. I like food," she explained to Max. "It's sort of my life, and I just enjoy it." Then she stuffed another bite of bread in her mouth to illustrate.

"She grew up in the bakery," Nate explained, trying not to smile at the look on Max's face as he watched Jessie devour her roll.

"The one you work at?" Max said.

"Well, I usually tell people that I came of age there," she explained. "I grew up in Colorado with my parents, and then they moved to Germany and left me to live with my uncle and cousin in the bakery. It's kind of a long story. But I spent some formative years there, yes."

NATALIE CHARLES

Max reached for his ice water and took a long sip.
Then he set it down carefully and nodded at Emily. "How
about you? Don't you work at the bakery, too?"

"Yes." She smiled. "But I also like to run. Did you
really run fifteen miles today?"

"Almost sixteen," Max said.

"Wow. I don't think I could ever run that far. I
completed a half marathon once, and I nearly collapsed at
the end."

"Look, it's real easy," Max said. "You've got to get 'I
can't do it' out of your head and go for it. You want to
push to the brink of death, but no further."

Nate and Jessie exchanged a glance over the flicker of
the candlelight. Jessie choked on a laugh and covered her
mouth with her napkin. Nate looked away and to the
floor, biting his lower lip. Fortunately, the soup course
came, and they were able to focus on that while Max gave
Emily advice that he promised would change her life.

By the time dessert came, it was clear that Jessie and
Max were not a love connection. For one thing, he
ordered black coffee, and she ordered the caramel turtle
cheesecake. For another, he and Emily seemed to *really* be
hitting it off. All's well that ends well, she thought, and
fished in her wallet for a few bills to cover her part of the
tab. "I'm going to run to the ladies' room," she said.

Emily stood. "I'll come with you."

The bathrooms were tiny, with two black stalls and
white-and-gray spotted granite counters. When they got

there, Emily sighed and leaned back against the dark purple wall. "I'm so confused. I need your advice."

"Mine? Really?" Jessie was kind of honored. Flummoxed, but honored.

"I just..." Emily tilted her head to the side. "I don't think Nate had a good time. He didn't talk very much."

Jessie checked her makeup in the mirror. No raccoon eyes. Victory. "I wouldn't take that personally. He gets that way when he's hungry."

Emily chewed her lower lip and folded her arms across her chest. "Do you think he'd be upset if we didn't go out again? I know you two are friends, and I don't want it to be weird. He's super nice," she added.

Jessie hoped Emily couldn't read the relief on her face. "Nate would definitely understand. He gets rejected all the time."

Emily blinked. "Oh. Okay." She nodded. "That's good, then. Max seems nice, doesn't he?"

She reached out and touched Emily's wrist. "Max is a great guy. And I think he likes you."

"Really?" Emily's eyes lit. "I think he's hot."

"Totally," Jessie said, and tried not to think about his feet. "Maybe you two will see each other again. Now, if you'll excuse me, my bladder's about to burst."

When she emerged from the stall, Jessie was a little surprised to see that Emily hadn't waited for her. She was also surprised that Nate was outside of the restroom, standing in the entrance to the rooftop. He watched her as she approached. "We've been rejected," he said.

A strand of Nate's hair fell against his eyebrow. He'd undone another button of his shirt, and his jeans skimmed his muscular legs in all the right ways. He was tall and strong and sexy as all hell. Jessie took him in and wondered how she could have ever missed it.

"How tragic," she breathed.

"I'm all broken up inside. Max and Emily are grabbing drinks," he smiled. "I'll take you home."

Jessie dropped her keys into his hand. "You walked?"

"Yeah. I'm not going to lie: I planned to be completely unattractive to Emily so I'd get to drive Old Cobalt again."

"You should've told me your plan."

"Why, so you could be unattractive to Max?" He shrugged. "I figured that part would come naturally."

"Hey!" She punched him playfully in the side. "That's mean."

"I'm kidding! You know that. I wanted to spend time with you, that's all."

She laughed, but it was subdued. Her throat was too tight, her thoughts elsewhere. "Thanks," she whispered.

At least the car started, and they pulled up to the cottage after a short, silent ride. Nate cut the engine. The full moon illuminated the interior of the vehicle, leaving few shadows. It even seemed to capture the unspoken words between them. Jessie wondered if Nate could hear the thrumming of her heart. Finally, he pulled the keys out of the ignition and said, "It's late. We don't have to run tomorrow morning if you don't want to."

"Tomorrow's my day to sleep in. I don't have to be at Hedda's until eight."

He shook his head. "The hours you keep. I don't know how you do it."

He clenched the keys in his fist once, twice. Then he handed them over to her and whispered, "I'm glad you're not Max's type."

He looked at her, and the breath caught in her throat. She wanted him like she'd never wanted anyone — or anything — in her life. "I'm sorry Emily isn't interested in you. She's always had a thing for guys with missing toenails."

But he didn't laugh. Instead he leaned across the console and cupped her chin carefully in his hands. "I could never date her." He stroked the pads of his thumbs across her cheeks. "I've gone on lots of dates and they've never amounted to anything, and it's because the entire time I'm with those women, I'm thinking about you."

His breath, sweet and minty, fell against her face with each word. She swallowed. "That's the best thing anyone's ever said to me."

He brought his thumbs down to the corners of her lips. Then he kissed her — softly at first, and then urgently, running his fingers across her bare shoulders and down her back. Jessie gripped his shirt and pulled at him. She wanted to be closer. She needed all of him. "Don't say anything," she said breathlessly when their kiss finally broke. "Come inside."

He did as she asked. No words, no lights other than the moonlight. No thoughts of how the morning would be. The first time, he took her slowly, almost reverently. The second time, with a frenzied need. The third time, well.

That was the time Jessie proved to him that she was the kind of girl who knew how and where to use her teeth. She brought him to his knees.

When she opened her eyes the next morning and realized the curtains were still open, Jessie's first thought was that they'd had sex in front of an open window. Her second was that she didn't care.

I had sex with Nate. The thought sent electricity coursing through her veins. He was still in bed beside her, naked and sleeping softly on her pillow. Her heart surged.

It shouldn't have been perfect. It should have been strange, and awkward, and uncomfortable. But instead of all of those things, it felt like a foregone conclusion. A little bit like destiny.

She crept out of bed and found a bathrobe. She wanted to make him breakfast — had she remembered to go grocery shopping that week? Jessie opened the refrigerator and was relieved to see a carton of eggs. She set them on the counter before grabbing the cream and butter. When a person rocks your world, there should be a decent breakfast afterward.

She melted the butter in a skillet, then cracked some eggs into a bowl, added some cream, salt, and pepper, and scrambled the mixture. She thought she'd seen some herbs in the vegetable drawer, but those would be a bonus. While she waited for the eggs to cook, she made a strong pot of coffee. Then she leaned against the counter, chewed on her thumbnail, and considered the fact that Nate was in her bed, very asleep, and very naked.

Holy crap.

She could tell Wren, but what should she *say*? What was going on, exactly? Maybe he'd wake up and tell her that they were better as friends. Hand to heaven, she would throw the eggs at him if he dared pull that. She was not a casual sex kind of girl. Not as a rule, anyway.

Jessie sat on her couch and drew her legs up. She was thinking too much, and she could try losing herself in home shopping or a cooking show of some sort. Then she heard a rustle in the bedroom, and her heart seized. She selected a channel and rose to her feet just in time to see Nate stumble into the kitchen. His hair was messy, and he was wearing only his jeans. And his boxer shorts, because she could see the black waistband sticking out. His abs. They belonged on a billboard.

Wow. Did she have good taste or what?

"Good morning," she said.

"'Morning." He smiled lazily and stretched. Then he reached into his pocket, pulled out a few bills, and set them on the counter. "That's from last night."

Breakfast smelled great. Scrambled eggs and coffee. Nate had woken up with his stomach growling. "Can I help you with anything?"

He scratched at his bare ribs and waited for a response. When he was hit with silence, he turned his head. "Jess?"

She was still there, all right. And she was glaring at him. "What's that for?" she growled, and pointed to the money. "What kind of person do you think I am?"

He rubbed his forehead. "I'm sorry. I paid your part of the tab last night. That's the money you put down at Sam's. I'm just giving it back." He forced a laugh. "Things can only go uphill from here, right?"

Jessie's shoulders relaxed, and her eyes softened. "Oh. Sorry. That was about to be very disappointing for me."

She tucked her blonde hair behind her ears and folded her arms. Her curls had turned to waves, and she had smudges of eye makeup on her lower lids. She looked a little tired, but neither of them had slept very well. He could watch her all day.

"What?" She looked down and away from him, then wiped at her cheeks. "Do I have something on my face?"

"No."

"Then why are you smiling at me?"

"I'm thinking that you're the prettiest girl I've ever seen."

She smiled but looked down again, too embarrassed to respond. Then she crossed the kitchen toward the stove. "You can go sit on the couch if you want. I have the fireplace channel on."

A video of a crackling fire played on the television screen. "That's a nice touch," he said.

"I should've had that idea first, to play a fire on a television channel all day. That's a million-dollar idea, I bet."

"It's gotta be close."

He couldn't help but smile. He loved that her idea of romance included a pre-recorded fire.

Instead of sitting in front of the video fire, he pulled out a stool at the breakfast bar and waited while Jessie scooped eggs onto two plates and poured two cups of coffee. She smiled sweetly as she handed him his breakfast, then she walked around the counter to sit beside him. "I like having you here," she said. "It's better than talking to Travis."

"High praise." He leaned over and kissed her on the temple. "I like being here. I'm sorry I made you feel like a prostitute just then."

"Not even a high-class one," she murmured as her gaze fell on the bills. "For future reference, I'm worth more than that."

"Amen," he said, and reached for his fork.

CHAPTER THIRTEEN

IN ALL OF the months he'd been training Claire, he'd never been late — until that day. When he pulled up in the driveway, she was on the front steps, tapping her watch. "Ten minutes late," she called as he stepped out of the car. "Don't think I'll forget it."

That morning, Claire was in a red tank and matching spandex shorts. The outfit left virtually nothing to the imagination. "I'm only eight minutes late," Nate said calmly. Claire was giving him a hard time. He knew her schedule was her own, and she didn't care.

"I have a knot in my shoulders," she said as she approached, rubbing at the base of her neck. "I was wondering whether you have any suggestions for a good massage therapist."

See? She was already on to a different topic. "I know a few good ones in the area. I'll give you their names."

"Bless you," she sighed, and took a sip of her tea. "Oh, and that reminds me: why are you so hard to get an appointment with these days? Should I take it personally?"

He winced. He'd been meaning to talk to Claire about a few things, and he'd been sort of avoiding her calls so that he could address her in person. "I'm making some changes. I've been teaching yoga at the Archer Cove Country Club, and the classes have been full. It's going well."

She stared at him blankly. "You. Teaching yoga. At a country club." Statements, not questions. "What the hell possessed you to do that?"

Okay, that wasn't exactly the supportive response he'd been anticipating. Wasn't Claire one of his biggest fans? "My buddy is the recreation director there, and one of his teachers broke an ankle a few days before the class started, so I filled in."

Nate realized that he could continue talking, but no amount of words was going to change that dismayed look on Claire's face. "Nate. Nate. Wait a sec, I'm trying to process this." She shut her eyes and took a deep breath, then opened them again and set a hand on his forearm. "You're telling me that I can't get extra appointments with you because you're doing head stands at the country club?"

"Head stands are an advanced move. This is more of an introductory —"

"Oh, this is bull." Claire turned around to talk to no one behind her. Then she spun around again, her arms spread wide. "If you needed extra money, you should've come to me. You didn't need to take some terrible job at

210

a country club. For God's sake. Do you like yoga, is that what it is? Because if you do, I can get you hired on private yachts. Would you like to do that, to go vacationing with people as their private — what are they called? Yogurts?"

"Yogis."

"Yes. Quick trip. You go somewhere nice, make a lot of money, do some yoga on the beach, and then come back and help me to get rid of my muffin top. Would you like something like that? "

That actually sounded terrible. "No, but thank you. I kind of like working there. At the country club. And it looks like they have an opening for the recreation director position."

The blood drained from her face. "Don't say it." She covered her ears: one with her hand, one with her thermos. "Don't. I can't stand the thought of you selling your soul to a golf course."

"I'm thinking about applying," he said. "Come on. It's nine to five. Good benefits, decent salary."

She stared at him, eyes wide and mouth open. "I can't even —" She waved a hand at him and turned to walk away. "Do you think this is funny, Nathan? I've lost five percent body fat in the past six months, and now you're telling me that you're going to give all of this up to plan racquetball tournaments? Why don't you just shove a chocolate croissant in my face while you're at it?"

Okay, this was new. Claire was legitimately worked up about his possible gig. This move was supposed to be about making him respectable and stable. It was supposed to be about advancement options — weren't those good things? He waved his hand at his SUV. "What am I doing now, Claire? I drive around and teach people how to make their push-ups more challenging, or how to do a squat without blowing out their knees. Where do I go from here? I can't advance, and I'm too young to be okay with doing this for the rest of my life."

She came back to center and took a breath, considering the statement. "I'm sorry," she said after a few moments had passed. "Of course. It's not just about me and my muffin top."

He exhaled. "Thank you for understanding."

"I understand nothing," she replied. "You don't belong in that country club — are you kidding me? You'd be miserable."

He shoved his hands in his pockets. "So what's your suggestion, then?"

She lifted her shoulders and said, "Easy. You're going to open a gym. I'm going to be your number-one investor."

"Claire." Nate rubbed at the back of his neck. His day had been going so damn well, and now it was all awkward. "I appreciate that. I really do. To be honest, I've been looking into the possibility of opening a gym, but there are some barriers."

She listened attentively as he detailed his discussions with George Dinardo and told her about the space. She asked thoughtful questions that indicated she knew a few things about running a business — questions about tax deductions and depreciations, returns on investment, and capitalization. Before he knew it, they were both leaning against the hood of the SUV, deep in conversation as the morning sun grew warmer.

"I'm going to be frank," Claire said at a pause in the conversation. "I want to invest in your gym. Not out of charity, but out of faith that you're going to make me a shit ton of money."

Nate laughed softly, feeling the conflict within him. On the one hand, he agreed with Claire: he could open a gym, and he could kick ass. On the other hand, there was always the possibility he could fail, and he didn't want to do that to Claire.

She sensed his hesitation. "You're not going to do this, are you? You're going to take that terrible country club job instead." She shook her head sadly. "Sorry to say, I'm not about to give up on you. I know you can do this, and I'm going to keep pushing you."

Nate stared down at his feet, wondering what he was so afraid of, anyway. Well, maybe it was just that he was used to being a lone wolf, doing his own thing without having anyone else depend on him. "The last thing I want is to let you down."

"Hey." Claire reached over to put a hand on his shoulder, but the look in her eyes was serious, not sympathetic. "You've never let me down. You're so thoughtful, I doubt you've ever let anyone down in your entire life. How about taking something for yourself this time? You never know, you may like getting what you actually want."

His thoughts flew to Jessie and quickly turned graphic. Yeah, he liked it, all right. Nate cleared his throat. "Okay. Let's say, for argument's sake, that I'm willing to keep an open mind about...what is this? A partnership?"

"I could be persuaded to be a silent investor *or* a silent partner."

"All right. You seem like you have some experience with these things. Let's assume I don't. So." He looked at her. "What's the plan?"

Claire grinned and linked her arm with his. "How much time do you have before your next client?"

"I'm free until noon."

"Then let's keep the workout light and talk shop in my kitchen. I do my best plotting over tea."

Normally, Jessie loved working with her family. On days that she came to work after a night of being shagged silly, however, she felt a little strange about the whole thing.

"Hey, Jess," Uncle Hank called from the kitchen. "Can you get me some bananas?"

Bananas. They were a harmless fruit — so why did her mind choose to go dirty? By the time she reached the kitchen with the bunch, her cheeks were enflamed and she couldn't look her uncle in the eyes.

Jeez. It's not like she'd been a virgin! Maybe she wasn't the most experienced person in the world, and maybe her last boyfriend hadn't been exactly attentive in that department, and perhaps there had been a long, long

214

dry spell before that...Still, sex had never made her lose her damn mind before. Though she'd never had sex like *that*, either.

Gosh. Nate had played her like a harp, knowing when to apply pressure and when to go gently. He took full control, and she loved every second of it. And the more she thought about him, the hotter she became, and the hotter she became, the more she giggled at menu items in Hedda's like "sweet nut rolls" and "hot buns." Because apparently sex with Nate made her a ten-year-old girl.

She needed a distraction. Fortunately, Emily was working, as well. "Did you have fun last night, Em?" Jessie asked during an afternoon lull. She could guess the answer, because Emily had misbuttoned her shirt for the first time ever, and had screwed up two lunch orders. If Jessie had to guess, Emily was giggling at bananas, too.

"Dinner was great," Emily said coyly.

"And how about drinks? Didn't you and Max stay?"

Yep, there it was! Emily looked away and pretended to be excruciatingly interested in a spot on the counter. "Drinks were great. I think Sam's has the best bartenders in town, don't you?" She licked her lips before looking back at Jessie. "Did you and Nate head home?"

"Yes. I mean, no. I drove him to my home and then he went to his place. Oh, wait!" Jessie smacked her forehead. "I meant, I drove him to his place and then went home. Alone."

Emily nodded thoughtfully as if the answer had made sense. "Did you watch that home shopping channel? I have to see those knives."

"It was a great set of knives. I'll get them for you when you graduate med school, how's that?"

"Deal."

Jessie could barely contain her excitement. Emily and Max! She was going to have to dig deeper, though closed-lipped Emily would be a tough nut to crack.

Nut. Heh.

To keep the impure thoughts at bay, Jessie spent the rest of the afternoon making cherry cordials and washing the bakery windows. Fortunately, she wasn't doing a good job with the windows. If she had been, she might not have noticed George Dinardo walking toward the bakery. She was out the door in two seconds flat. "Hi, Mr. Dinardo!" She waved eagerly.

Jessie knew that look. She'd seen it often. It was a special blend of confusion and desire to not look confused. Mr. Dinardo lifted his hand and gave a guarded smile. "Why, hello."

He has no idea who I am. "I'm Jessie Mallory. Hank Mallory's niece."

Recognition crossed his face. "Oh, yes. Sorry, I must've had the sun in my eyes. I couldn't see your face at first."

"That's all right. Are you going somewhere? You look like you're busy."

"I was heading to the bookstore."

She folded her hands demurely. "Do you have a few minutes? I wanted to talk to you about the space you have for rent."

He agreed and followed her back into Hedda's. Had she been thinking, Jessie's heart would have been in her throat. This was her one chance to make an impression. Screw that up, and her dreams of opening "Chocolate Crush" were as good as ended. Fortunately, Jessie had put her brain on neutral and started coasting. The words came effortlessly.

"I have a line of chocolates that I'd like you to try," she said, and rounded the chocolate display case to the back. "Which do you prefer, milk chocolate or dark?"

"Milk, please."

Jessie lifted a shiny white confectioner's box, added a pink and white polka-dotted sheet of tissue paper, and began adding chocolates. She chose a few of her favorites: a creamy hazelnut crème truffle, a sea salted caramel, rocky road bark, and toasted coconut squares. "I make them right here, all by hand."

Mr. Dinardo took a small bite of the coconut square and chewed it thoughtfully. "Delicious. The chocolate is wonderful."

"Isn't it? It took me ages to select the right chocolate, but it was worth it. Here, I'll show you how I made those."

As he sampled the sweets, Jessie took him on a tour of the kitchen, showing him the molds and the cooling racks, and how she tempered the chocolate bars to keep them at the right consistency. "I make everything the old-fashioned way," she explained. "I use these marble slabs to make toffee."

Mr. Dinardo glanced around the kitchen. "You don't have a lot of room back here."

Jessie took a breath. "Well, that's kind of what I wanted to talk to *you* about."

She explained that she was looking for a storefront, a small place to set up her own shop and expand. She told him about her sales numbers and how her business was growing slowly but steadily. The more she talked, the more he listened. He even nodded his head at the right times.

"So although I think I could afford to rent a space for the price you're asking," she said, "the size of the space will be the determining factor."

Mr. Dinardo took another bite of the hazelnut crème truffle and chewed slowly. "Are you asking me to divide the deli space?"

Don't look like you're begging! She calmly nodded her head. "I would love to wall off a small section of the space, maybe at the corner so I have more window room. I've considered the layout, and I really think that it can be done in a way that won't hurt your ability to rent the remaining space. Here, I'll show you."

Jessie grabbed a pen and a small pad of paper and rendered the deli in a series of slash marks and cross-hatches. "See, if you place the wall here, then that gives access to a portion of the kitchen but leaves a larger section open."

He peered over her shoulder. "But won't you need more kitchen space than that?"

"I'd extend the kitchen out to about here," she said. "What I need is some additional work space, but I wouldn't be bringing large equipment." She smiled. "It's just me."

Mr. Dinardo lifted the drawing gently from her hands and pulled a pen out of his pocket. He set to work making calculations as to the remaining square footage. "I wouldn't even consider this if we hadn't had so much feedback about the space being difficult," he said. "It's not quite right for a restaurant or office space, and it's too large for the average store that would locate in the center of Archer Cove."

She waited breathlessly as he studied the drawing, turning it in his hands to study it from different angles. Finally, he said, "Your chocolate is delicious."

He stopped. *No!* Jessie bit her lower lip and waited for him to deliver the bad news.

"I'd love to have you in that space."

Wait...what? Mr. Dinardo clicked the pen closed and put it back into his pocket. Jessie felt light-headed. "What's the condition?"

He paused. "The what?"

"The condition. You said you'd love to have me in that space. But what's the condition?"

Mr. Dinardo looked puzzled. "You'd have to pay rent, of course."

Jessie clapped her hands across her mouth. "That's all? I'd have to pay rent? Nothing else?"

"You'd be responsible for construction costs."

She nodded quickly. "Yes, I've applied for a loan to cover all of that. I just can't — this is unbelievable!"

She'd done it. She'd actually done it! George Dinardo was going to divide the space, and she was going to have a storefront with a pink and white polka-dot awning and scrolling letters on the windows. All because she had sold him on the idea.

"Mr. Dinardo, I could kiss you right now."

He laughed and held up a hand. "That's fine. We'll seal the deal the old-fashioned way and write up a contract."

"Is there anything I can do to say thank you?" She looked at the almost-empty box in his hands. "How about a larger box of chocolates for the family?"

He smiled. "My wife would love that. She'll be so happy to hear that a chocolate shop is coming to Archer Cove. She has a sweet tooth."

"Well, we'll have to send you home with a lot of sweets, then."

By the time George Dinardo left, it was time to lock up. Jessie stayed to bake for a while and then left for home. She decided on the way that she wasn't going to breathe a word about her business until that loan came through. The agreement with Mr. Dinardo wasn't final until she had the money she needed to invest, and there was no sense getting too excited just yet — she was overstimulated as it was.

Her stomach was filled with pins and prickles — over her business and over Nate. Just a few weeks ago when Quinn had dumped her, she'd felt stunned. Humiliated.

Now she felt hopeful. Life was full of wonderful possibilities. It made her want to write poetry. Instead, she texted Nate.

Are you coming over later?

His response came almost instantly: *I hope that's an invitation. Be there at 6.*

Jessie didn't care that she was walking down the busy street, smiling at her cell phone like a woman possessed. Life was her favorite!

She stopped at the market and picked up a few ingredients for dinner before heading home. Then she took a long, hot bath and prepared a simple dinner for two: baked salmon with a honey mustard glaze, baked sweet potatoes, and a kale salad. Nate knocked on the door just as she was lighting a little tea candle she'd found mixed in with her Tupperware.

"You don't have to knock," she said as she swung open the door. "I let people who sleep with me just walk in —"

He stepped inside and pulled her against his chest, silencing her with a kiss that stole her breath. Then he pulled back to say, "I missed you all day long."

"I missed you, too." She sighed. His lips tickled her cheek and sent a shiver down her spine. "I made dinner."

"Perfect." He grinned wickedly and closed the door behind him with his foot. "I'll take care of dessert."

CHAPTER FOURTEEN

BY THE END of three weeks, Nate was practically living in the cottage. Jessie figured it was fair enough since he owned it. As a bonus, he refused to collect rent. "It's the perk of sleeping with the landlord," he explained. She'd take it.

There were other perks, too. Like having a person to talk to in the morning instead of Prince Travis, and having someone to curl up against at night. She was learning that Nate sometimes took too long in the shower, and at night he pulled the covers to his side. But he also gave great back rubs, so she could forgive him.

They still woke early in the mornings to run, and with the Sweet Relief 5K only two weeks away, Jessie was amazed that she could run for twenty minutes straight. She was even more amazed that she enjoyed running. On the rest days, her legs felt twitchy and restless. "I hope you're happy," she said one night as they cleared the dinner plates. "You've turned me into a damn runner."

Nate froze, a mock stunned expression on his face. "Jessica Mallory, other than first agreeing to have sex with me, that may be the best thing you've ever said." She'd thrown a dishtowel at him.

Mostly, Jessie walked around thinking that she was happier than she'd ever remembered being. She felt like she was wrapped in a soft blanket and then bubble wrapped for added warmth and protection from the elements. Yes, being with Nate felt like wearing rain boots; she still had some bad days, but they didn't penetrate in the same way.

Then there came the afternoon that she went out during her break to hang flyers advertising the "Sweet Relief 5K." She turned out of Hedda's Bakery and nearly ran smack-dab into Quinn. "Whoa!" he said, and grabbed her by the arms before she struck him. "Careful there!"

He was business casual in a pair of chinos and a red polo shirt, and he was wearing the same cologne he always wore. Jessie's hands flew to her heart, which was scampering like a bunny in her chest. She dropped the flyers across the sidewalk. "Sorry! I wasn't looking!"

"I'll say." But he was amused, not angry. He released her arms. "Are you all right?"

"Fine." She fell to her knees and gathered the flyers, which were already starting to blow down the street.

"Here, let me help you."

Between the two of them, they managed to collect all of the flyers before she lost them to the wind or to someone's careless footstep. Jessie clasped them in her arms. They were disordered, but at least they were still intact. "Thank you," she said.

"No problem. It was my fault, really." Quinn rose to his feet. "I was just going to grab some lunch, but I hadn't decided on where yet." He looked at the bakery.

It was all nonsense, of course. Hedda's was the best lunch place in a three-block radius, and Quinn knew that. And of course he knew that she'd be working there. It was almost as if he'd stopped by just to see her. Jessie's palms grew damp.

She'd lost track of how many weeks it had been since she'd last seen Quinn, and of course she was in a different place at the moment. A better place. So why did bumping into her ex-boyfriend feel like getting jolted with a cattle prod?

She lifted her shoulders in a way that she hoped signaled her complete disinterest. "Well, we have lunch here. I'm heading out for a walk, but Emily can help you."

Her casual words belied her swirling emotions, some of which threatened to bubble to the surface if they stood there much longer.

Quinn made no effort to hide his scrutiny of her. "You look good, Jess."

"I feel good," she said, not bothering to add that at that particular moment, she wasn't feeling so hot. "Nate and I have been running together. He's planning a 5K. You should run it." She handed him a flyer.

He chuckled at that and held the flyer by the corner, as if it was dirty. "I don't know about that. We'll see."

"Suit yourself. Enjoy your lunch."

She turned on her heel and managed to take one step before he grabbed her by the elbow and said, "Wait. I haven't seen you in a while. Do you want to grab lunch?"

"I already ate." She pulled her arm out of his grip, trying to be polite about it.

"Well." He stepped closer and put his hands in his pockets, giving her a grin. "Maybe I can help you with the flyers?"

No, she was sure she didn't need help with that. "You should get your lunch. I'm going to go — hey!"

Quinn grabbed a few flyers off the top of her stack and headed for the nearest utility pole. "Do you have tacks, or...wait, here's one." He pulled an old gold tack out of the wood and used it to hang the flyer." See? I can help."

Jessie's jaw tightened, and a plume of anger burst in her chest. "I didn't mean you weren't able to help. I meant that I didn't *want* your help."

She reached for the flyers in his hand, but he pulled them away and headed for the next pole. "Come on. I'll help you, and we'll get these hung in no time."

She watched him as he located an old tack on the next pole and hung the next flyer. But he hung it in an awkward location where it wouldn't get much visibility. Jessie's feet pounded on the cement as she went over to undo the damage. "You're doing it all wrong. Just let me —"

"I'm a senior associate at Emerson & Palmer. I close multimillion-dollar deals. You don't think I know how to hang flyers?"

"No, I don't." It took some effort to remove the tack, which he'd driven deep into the wood. Jessie picked at it with her nail, but it wouldn't budge. "Damn it, Quinn. No one's going to see this now."

He laughed, but it sounded dry and ugly, and it made her feel two feet tall. "How many flyers do you have here, fifty? I'm sure people will see at least one of them." He looked down at them for the first time. "Sweet Relief, huh? Sponsored by The Chocolate Crush? What's that?"

"It's my new business." She reached for the flyers in his hand, and once again he pulled them out of her reach. "Give those to me."

"You're starting a business now?" He smiled. "That's really adorable. I want to hear more about it. Let me guess: it involves polka dots, doesn't it?"

Since when was he such a condescending prick? Jessie's cheeks burned with rage, and the corners of her eyes started to prickle. Damn it, she didn't want to cry. Not in front of Quinn. But she couldn't get control of her anger at the moment. She couldn't talk, either. Her throat was clogged by emotion.

"I'm proud of you." Quinn's voice was slightly mocking as he wandered over to the next utility pole and searched for a tack. "I am. I didn't think you had it in you. But I guess I'll have to see it to believe it, right? I mean, leaving your Uncle Hank and the comfort of Hedda's, actually taking a leap." He shook his head. "I guess I'll be watching."

He looked at her and flashed a smug grin. All of the hurt, shame, and anger that Jessie thought she'd been managing so well flipped off something in her brain. The next thing she knew, she was nearly on top of him, tugging the flyers out of his hand. *Her* flyers. "Stop it!" she shouted. "Stop it! Stop it!"

"What, you want these?" He crinkled the flyers in his fist before flinging them on the sidewalk. "There. Happy?"

She picked them off the ground, but they were hopelessly wrinkled and torn. Still, Jessie smoothed them as best she could, hating the way her chin trembled. "What is it with you?" she hissed. "You can't handle being rejected? I don't want to hang flyers with you, so you try to ruin my day?"

He sneered down at her. "I don't get rejected, sweetheart. Not by you."

The barb stung, but she stood her ground and lifted her chin. "You're a small person, Quinn. Small people leave those around them feeling worse."

"Thanks for the psychobabble, Miss Chocolate Crush." He rolled his eyes. "Whatever. I try to do something nice for you, and this is what I get."

"No, you didn't try to do something nice for me. Not at all." Her voice shook with the force of her emotion, and she felt like the world was rippling straight through her. "You don't do nice things for people. You don't think of anyone but yourself."

God help her, she was crying. She couldn't hold back the flood. But she also couldn't hold on to that hurt and anger forever. She swallowed the lump in her throat, but her voice still cracked. "I thought I cared about you, and all you did was treat me like garbage. I thought that was my fault, that I wasn't good enough. Now I understand that our relationship was never about me. It was always about you."

He looked around them while she talked, feigning boredom. "Like I said, whatever. You're obviously hormonal right now."

She bit her lip and took a deep breath. The tears had started to subside. She wasn't going to give him the pleasure of hurting her. "I wish you the best, Quinn, but please don't ever try to contact me again. And don't come to Hedda's. You're not welcome there."

She pressed the flyers to her chest and returned to the little bakery. It felt safer there, and she could always hang the flyers after work.

When Nate returned to the cottage, Jessie was curled up in sweatpants on the couch, reading a book. "Hey," he said as he closed the door behind him.

"Hey."

She looked up with a little smile. Her eyes — had she been crying? She looked tired. Nate looked around the kitchen. "Want me to make dinner?"

"I'm not really hungry tonight. I thought I'd do some reading and go to bed early."

He paused. "Is everything okay?"

She closed her paperback slowly and lifted her head. "Just a long day. Nothing to worry about."

Nate had always known that Jessie worked long hours. She was up before dawn, and after she left the bakery, she worked on her own chocolates at home. Of course, they'd been pulling some late nights together, too. He figured it was beginning to catch up with her. "You should get some sleep," he said, and walked over to kiss her on the forehead. "I'll get out of your way. I should go home and do some laundry."

She intertwined their fingers, keeping him close. "You don't have to go. I like having you here."

He brushed her hair back from her face. Man, she looked exhausted. "Then I'll leave for a few hours and be back later. But I hope you're sleeping by then."

She smiled faintly. "Will do."

It was fine, Nate thought as he headed out again. Quinn had been texting him that afternoon, so they could meet up for dinner. They hadn't seen each other in weeks. After a series of text messages, they agreed to meet at Meme's. By the time Nate arrived, Quinn was already seated.

"Hey man," Nate said as he pulled up a chair. "Good to see you."

"You too." But Quinn didn't look happy to see Nate at all. In fact, he looked pissed off about something. Jeez, was there something in the water? "Bad day?"

His friend only grunted in response. "The usual."

"What's new? I don't see you much these days. You must be busy with Caryn."

Quinn eased back in his chair and looked away. "Caryn's a bitch," he said.

"Huh." An evening alone folding laundry was beginning to look better and better. Nate reached for the menu. "Should we get the usual?"

A waiter came by and set a pint of beer in front of Quinn. "Anything for you, sir?"

"Just a water is fine," Nate said.

Quinn took a long sip and set the glass back on the table. "I'm swearing off women."

He leaned forward and tapped Quinn's glass. "You know, you may want to think about swearing off this stuff, too. Not that I don't love getting drunk phone calls at one in the morning."

"Piss off. It's my first drink." Quinn eyed him sidelong. "What's going on?"

"With what?"

"With you. You look happy about something, and I want to know what it is."

Nate and Jessie hadn't told anyone about their relationship yet. Not that it was a secret. More like they didn't want to name it. They hadn't had The Talk. But it was gnawing at Nate, and things between him and Quinn were going to be awkward all night if he wasn't straight with him. Besides, it wasn't like Quinn would be upset. He and Jessie had barely dated, and they'd broken up almost six weeks ago.

"It's funny, actually," he said. "Jessie and I are starting to see each other."

Quinn's face showed no reaction. "See each other? What's that mean, you're sleeping together?"

There was an edge to his voice that Nate didn't like. "It's what I said. We're seeing each other. I wanted you to hear it from me first. I don't want things between us to be strange."

Quinn took another gulp of his beer. "Funny, 'cause she was all over my junk this afternoon."

Nate froze. "You saw each other? When?"

Damn, but he hated feeling like the jealous boyfriend all of a sudden. He wasn't that type. But Jessie and Quinn had a history, and she hadn't even mentioned seeing him.

"I was out at lunch and I ran into her," he said. "She was hanging flyers for that race you guys are doing. She asked me for my help."

Nate clenched his jaw as the image popped into his head: Quinn and Jessie hanging the race flyers together. "She didn't say anything to me."

His friend arched an eyebrow knowingly. "Yeah, well. It was nothing, so don't worry about it. I'm totally over it."

"And how was she?" He shouldn't have asked. He didn't want to know. It wasn't his business, and he trusted her. There was no reason not to.

"How was she?" Quinn echoed as he thought about it. "Friendly, I guess. Flirty. You know how Jessie is. She was wearing a cute little skirt. She has great legs."

Nate's stomach had worked itself into a ball. He didn't feel like eating. He was sick of Quinn and the way he treated people. He was sick of feeling like he had to compete with him for Jessie's attention. He thought back to that night that he'd accused Jessie of making a lot of excuses for Quinn. Well, he was no better.

"You know what, man? I'm not feeling that great tonight." Nate pushed back his chair. "I think I'm going to go home."

Quinn looked surprised. "Why, because of what I said about Jessie? I told you, I'm not interested."

Nate stood. "Yeah, you're not interested. And you only said something about her to get at me, and to try to put me in my place. I've looked at you as my equal, but you seem to think you're better. Friends like that suck."

He turned and walked out of the restaurant, into the early evening air. He told himself that he couldn't listen to Quinn. He may have been a friend once, but he hadn't been for a while. He wasn't a person who could be trusted, and he'd only said those things about Jessie to get under Nate's skin. But damn if it didn't gnaw at him all night.

He went back to his apartment and ran two loads of laundry. By the time they were dry, he told himself he was too tired to head back to Jessie's. He crawled into bed and felt his bones sink into the mattress, weary from the day.

CHAPTER FIFTEEN

JESSIE WOKE UP alone. It took a moment to register. Then she sat bolt upright in bed and looked at the space beside her. Nate's part of the bed was still made. A thread of panic worked through her as she fumbled for her cell. Thank goodness — he'd sent a text: *Fell asleep doing laundry.*

She exhaled. No big deal.

She showered, dressed, and walked to Hedda's. The morning was overcast, but the meteorologist predicted sunshine. After a good night's sleep, Jessie felt like a new person. That morning, her affirmation was different: *I am strong as hell.* Because she was. She'd stood up to Quinn, and as bad as it had felt to say those things to him, it was cathartic. Her life was full of possibilities, and Quinn was no longer one of them. Life was sweeter.

Jessie whistled to herself as she baked lemon poppy seed muffins and cinnamon rolls. She hummed as she swept the floors and cleaned the glass on the display cases. She would've danced around the kitchen if Uncle Hank hadn't told her numerous times that it was a no-dance zone. Nate had fallen asleep while doing laundry. He hadn't left her.

She was at the counter when Mr. White came into the bakery, looking exactly as a loan officer should in his pale blue tie and white short-sleeved starched shirt. "Good morning, Mr. White," she said cheerfully. "What can I get for you?"

"I'm actually here to talk to you about your application," he said. "Is this a good time?"

Jessie's heart stopped in its tracks. She took a quick glance around the bakery. "We're in the morning lull, so it should be fine."

"Great. We can sit at one of these tables, and if you get busy, you can just go right back to work."

He selected a table by the window, the one Jessie thought of as the "lovers' table," because of its size and privacy. She pulled out the white wrought-iron chair and took a seat on the blue cushion. Her heart was going a mile a minute, but this had to be good, right? Loan officers didn't come to tell people their application had been rejected...did they?

Mr. White opened a brown leather briefcase and extracted a manila envelope. "I've got good news and bad news," he said. "Which would you like first?"

Jessie swallowed. "The good news. Definitely."

He paused. "I'll give you the bad news first. It makes more sense, logically."

"But I thought —"

234

"The bank has rejected your loan application," he said.

"Oh." Her hands covered her heart. There was that ache. "Oh." Again. It took her breath with it.

"I'm sorry," he said. "But the good news is that we will approve a loan for you in this amount." He slid the paperwork across the table. Then he sat back and folded his hands.

Jessie blinked. There were so many numbers. Her eyes drifted down the page, over the figures she'd supplied, her address...she saw it. A number, and a dollar sign. "This?" She pointed to it. "That's the number?"

"That's the one. And the interest rate is right there. What do you think?"

It wasn't exactly what she'd hoped for, but if she worked with Dinardo and was smart about reducing the size of the space and making renovations...A smile spread across her face. "I can do this," she whispered. "I can make it work. Oh my gosh, I'm opening my own chocolate shop!"

Mr. White smiled. "I've seen your race flyers around town. I had to stop in a few days ago to try some of your chocolates. They're delicious. You have a very bright future ahead of you."

She was beaming. She couldn't help herself. "This is wonderful news. I'm so happy!" Without a thought, she rose from her seat and flung her arms around him. "Thank you so much! You're changing my life, Mr. White!"

He laughed stiffly and patted her back. "All right. You're welcome. If this figure works, then I'll get the loan finalized and you can have a check as early as next week."

"That's incredible. I can't thank you enough. Wait!" She darted behind the display case and piled a large box with assorted chocolates. "Please take these back to the bank, with my thanks."

"Thank you, Ms. Mallory. Have a great day."

"I will."

She waited until he'd left the bakery to shriek. The customers turned to stare. "I'm opening a chocolate shop!"

Emily came running from behind the counter, and Uncle Hank came out from the kitchen. "What happened?" he asked.

Jessie ran over to embrace him. "I'm opening my own chocolate shop, Uncle Hank!"

Emily squealed and joined the hug. "That's fantastic!"

"I'm so proud of you, Jess!" Uncle Hank said. When she looked up, he had tears in his eyes. "I knew you could do it."

Jessie's head swirled with possibilities. "I'll need an awning, and I have to buy some more equipment, and maybe I'll look online for display cases..."

"This is going to be so great," Emily said. "You should be proud of yourself. This is what you've wanted for years."

And Jessie decided that she was proud. She was finally becoming herself.

The counters and shelving were gone in the deli space, so Nate signed the lease by pressing the contract against the window. He got a few letters in before the ink in the pen stopped flowing. He shook the pen and laughed. "Someone's trying to stop me."

"Nope, no one's stopping you," George Dinardo said. "It's all yours."

Claire stood by, a white handbag dangling from her folded arms. "This space is absolutely perfect," she gushed. "I'm going to get my contractors in here on Monday. We'll be up and running in no time flat."

It was all happening so fast that Nate felt light-headed. When George Dinardo had called and told him that he was thinking of splitting the space in half, Nate knew he had to act or lose his chance for good. For her part, Claire was eager to invest, and she'd even managed to talk down the price significantly by offering to sign a three year lease.

"If I can only sign my name," he said. He knelt on one knee and balanced the contract on the other. "There we go. Much better."

"Excellent." George held out his hand. "I'll get copies of this to you in a few days. It's been a pleasure."

"Same here. Thanks, Mr. Dinardo."

Claire patted him on the back. "How's it feel? You've got a space and three years to make it work."

He set his hands on his waist. "It's gonna work, partner."

He had too many ideas to count. Equipment to purchase, training programs to test. There were hundreds of possibilities, all of them great. He couldn't wait to tell Jessie.

As upset as he'd been the night before, he'd felt better in the morning. Of course he could trust Jessie. The last role he wanted to play was that of a jealous boyfriend. She deserved better than that. Quinn had only been pressing his buttons.

When he called her, it sounded like she'd had a great day, too. "I can't wait to talk to you!" she gushed.

Nate smiled. Her happiness was contagious. "Same here. See you at home at six?"

"I love that you called the cottage 'home.' See you then!"

He stopped to buy her a bouquet of pink and white sweetheart roses, feeling as shaky as a teenager on his first date. This was it. Tonight he was going to tell her how he felt, lay it all on the line. *I love you. I've always loved you.* He wondered if he'd be able to get the words out in the way he needed to: loud and clear, so there'd be no doubt. The last thing he wanted Jessie to feel was any doubt. She'd been hurt enough in her life. *I'm yours for as long as you want me to be.*

He was nearly giddy as he walked up the front path to the little blue cottage, the bouquet behind his back. Jessie swung open the front door, looking as beautiful as ever in a white dress with pink ribbon woven around the waist. He could tell she was bursting. "Hello, gorgeous." He brought out the flowers. "These are for you."

238

"They're beautiful! Thank you!" She kissed him on the lips and tightened a hand around his tie. "I missed you."

"I missed you too."

"Oh, I can't even stand it!" She stepped back and announced, "I'm opening a chocolate shop! I was approved for a loan today!"

"What?" Nate shook his head. "That's unbelievable! I mean, not unbelievable. It's completely believable because you're incredible. Sweetie, congratulations!" He pulled her into his arms.

"I'm so happy, Nate! It's like my life is finally coming together!" She stepped back and smelled the roses. "I'm going to find a vase. Come inside."

He watched her as she nearly skipped around the kitchen, looking through the cabinets. She found a white vase above the refrigerator. "I had no idea all of this was going on," he said. "You know how to keep a secret."

"A surprise." She beamed. "I didn't want to say anything until it was official, but I have a space and everything." She clapped her hands together. "I thought I was going to be afraid to make this change, but it feels so perfect. I know I'm ready for it."

"You found a space?" Nate plucked a green grape from a bunch in the fruit bowl on the counter. "Whereabouts?"

"The Dinardo's Deli space! I spoke with Mr. Dinardo a few weeks ago, and he agreed to split the unit in half." She puffed her chest. "Looks like I'm quite the negotiator."

He stopped mid-chew. "Wait. What?"

Jessie unwrapped the roses from the green tissue paper and brought them to the sink. "I'm getting the Dinardo's Deli space. Nate, I can't thank you enough for showing it to me when you did. The more I thought about it, the more I thought it was perfect, and I'm going to get the side with all of the windows. It's going to be brilliant."

He swallowed the grape after two chews and felt it skim down his esophagus. He was going to be sick. "Jess. We should talk."

"That's right, you have news, don't you?" She looked over her shoulder. "And here I've been blabbing away."

Crap. He leaned one arm against the counter and told himself that they would figure it out somehow. It would be okay, but he had to tell her. She had to hear it from him first. "I'm opening a gym." It came out as a mumble.

"What?" She spun from the sink. "I'm so proud of you! This is a big day! Have you thought about financing? Because I've been through the lending process —"

"Yeah, I've thought about financing." He righted himself and waited for the courage to say what had to come next. "I've signed a lease already. Just signed it, in fact."

"Wow, Nate." She giggled uneasily. "Talk about keeping secrets. Where's the space?"

Here goes. "It's the Dinardo space, actually."

There was a stretch of silence as the news settled. Jessie's smile slowly fell from her face. "You mean you're renting the other half?"

Hopeful to the end. Nate inhaled. "No. I'm renting all of it. For three years." When he saw the look of anguish, he hated that he was the cause. "It's not my fault. I had no idea you were looking at that space. You never told me about any of this!"

"I was trying to accomplish something on my own. You knew that," she said, her voice splintering. "You knew that I wanted to open a chocolate shop, and that's the only space in town!" The rims of her eyes grew red. "How could you do that to me?"

Anger boiled in his chest. He'd been her friend when she was at her lowest. How many times had he dropped everything and come running, just because she needed him to drive her home, or try her fudge, or eat pizza with her? How dare she accuse him of intentionally hurting her? "I've always put you first. Believe it or not, I started thinking about opening a gym because I wanted you to be proud of me. I wanted you to see me for once. Me, not Quinn." He tried his best to keep his tone measured, but his chest was breaking wide open just then, and it hurt like hell. "I've always thought of you. I guess we both have."

Her eyes widened and then narrowed. "What does that mean?"

"You spend a lot of time thinking about yourself. Numbing your pain with sugar and alcohol. How about dealing with life head-on, Jess? It's not always roses. My dad died when I was thirteen years old. You think that's easy to cope with?" His fists were clenched so tightly they hurt. "Do you think I had a friend to hold my hand and take long walks with? Someone to string along while I waited for something better to come by?"

Her mouth opened. "Wait for something better to come by? What are you talking about?"

"I know you saw Quinn yesterday. I know you spent time with him, and that you didn't tell me about it. So tell me: am I just another part of your plan? Another accomplishment to make you more attractive? Drop fifteen pounds and have sex with Quinn's best friend? Is that how you get to be an Emerson & Parker wife these days?"

He knew as soon as the words flew out of his mouth that this was a low blow. Her chin shook and she looked down and away. Her hands were lying on the counter, palms up with her fingers open. He'd cut too deeply. He'd gone too far. "Jess. Wait." Nate's voice softened by a degree. "Let's talk about this —"

A tear rolled down her cheek and she wiped it away. "Please go." The request was barely a whisper.

"I don't want to. I don't want to leave things between us like this."

She turned her gaze to him, and he saw the anguish and the hurt. This is what happens when you know everything about a person, he thought. You know exactly how to hurt them. He'd taken a cheap shot, and he hated himself for it. "Please. Can we talk about this?"

Tears spilled from her eyes and splattered on the dark gray granite countertops. She didn't even move to wipe them. "I trusted you," she said, her voice eerily calm. "Please go, and please don't come back."

He couldn't look at her any more, knowing that he'd only see pain in her face. If leaving made her feel better, there wasn't a choice.

Nate turned without another word and headed for the door. Silently, quickly, regretfully.

CHAPTER SIXTEEN

SO, LIFE HAD taken a little bit of a nosedive, and Jessie didn't even have ice cream in her freezer. Like the day could get any worse.

She broke the stems of the roses and threw the blooms in the trash. Then she took her foot and stomped them down, smashing eggshells, vegetable peelings, and a rotten apple she'd thrown away earlier. Her shoes were dirty and smelled like garbage, and she hated the world with every fiber of her being.

How could life be so cruel, to set her up for such a colossal disappointment? To think she could have spent so many hours on that stupid loan application, pulling together sales data and putting it into a colorful chart, only to find out that her best friend had taken the only available space — the *perfect* space — right out from under her! The more she thought about how trusting she'd been, how optimistic...she was a fool. Her mistake was in being vulnerable enough to get hurt.

For a long time she stood in her kitchen and looked around her cottage, at the silly, pointless life she'd constructed. She had a little rental cottage and a taxidermic fox for company. She gave her heart out to careless men. Despite her best efforts, life was continuing to run on schedule and leaving her behind.

She didn't know how long she stood there, feeling sorry for herself. Maybe she did numb her feelings. If Nate were half as sensitive, he'd want to numb himself, too. But she was trying to change, and she had. She wasn't going to start taking backward steps. Not now.

Without thinking, she went into her bedroom and changed out of her dress and into a pair of running shorts and a T-shirt. She laced up her shoes and headed outside, where the evening was still bright. Her heart hurt. Her head told her that she was terrified and ashamed. But she could still run.

She ran harder than she'd run before. She took the hills. She ran until her legs hurt and her lungs burned, and then she kept going, remembering Max telling her to *push to the brink of death, but no further*. She ran until she couldn't hear her mind repeating the things Nate had said to her. Over to the copse of pines, down the dusty path to the clearing, then to the secret beach that he'd shown her. She was claiming it as her own. She was claiming her life as her own.

I am good enough.

She whispered it out loud and allowed the waves to carry it out to sea, feeling certain that this wasn't a statement that would sink to the bottom of the ocean. As long as she continued to say it, people would hear it. *I am Jessica Mallory, and I am good enough.* The world needed to know.

The sun was setting by the time she turned and headed back. Her legs were too weary to run any more, so she walked home. She didn't greet Travis or turn on the television. Instead, she took a long, hot shower and sobbed into the spray. Then she dried off, dressed, and crawled into bed. Her last thought as she drifted off to sleep was that she would come through. She would not be the cat lady, or a recluse. She was hurting, but it would pass, and then she would be stronger.

Jessie fell asleep determined to wake up the next morning, and to try to love life again.

Nate didn't come to her house the next morning for a run. Or the day after that, or the day after that. Jessie took comfort in routine, and slowly the bruise across her heart stopped aching so intensely. But she wasn't pretending, either. When Emily asked her how Nate was doing, Jessie replied, "We aren't speaking to each other right now."

Poor Emily. She really did look flustered at that, and she tucked her hair behind her ears and apologized. Jessie touched her arm lightly and said, "It's okay. You didn't know."

"I always manage to push the wrong buttons," she said.

"You ask questions, that's all." Jessie returned to her work, slicing honeydew melon into plastic to-go containers. "Are things with Max going well?"

"Eh." Emily lifted her shoulders. "He'll be heading out on missions soon, and he doesn't want to be tied down. His words. It's one of those things that was fun while it lasted."

"Look at you, all resilient." Jessie was impressed. She'd never been the type, herself.

"It's not love," Emily said as she poured water into the coffee maker. "He's a nice guy and everything, and we've had some interesting talks, but I can't see us together. When I'm with him, I don't feel like I'm special. Just another person to talk to about his toenails."

Jessie giggled. She'd always liked Emily.

Mostly, Jessie was holding up and putting on a good show. Every now and then she had to remind herself that she couldn't text Nate. Like when she was watching home shopping and that knife set was offered (she bought three sets: one for herself, one for the bakery, and one for Emily). Or like when her peanut butter fudge came out *amazing*. Or when she ran down to that secret beach again, half-hoping he'd be there even though he wasn't, and she missed him. There were just things she couldn't tell him anymore, and that made her sad. But she couldn't change the entire world, only her corner.

She picked up a few items at the market on her way home from work. That evening's plans were simple. Wren had sent her an ebook that she swore would lift her spirits. "It's a novella called *To Thrill a Cockingbird*," she'd gushed. "It's about this guy who strips his way through law school, and it's completely smutty. You'll love every word."

"I hope there's an impassioned speech about justice," Jessie said.

"No chance. But there's this one scene that — let's just say you'll never look at a tube of toothpaste the same way again."

Sold! Jessie intended to settle down with a cup of tea and read it that very night. But first: dinner with her parents.

Jessie had called them the evening before and invited them over to dinner so that she could share her news with them in person. She was going to prepare a kale salad with grilled chicken, diced apples, blue cheese, and butternut squash, all drizzled with a balsamic vinaigrette. She turned on the radio and set to work preparing the meal and setting the little table. There was a small brick patio in back where they could sit and enjoy the sunset, and Jessie had a small plate of chocolates for dessert. In her mind, she rehearsed the evening.

Mom and Dad. I'm opening my own business.

Sadie would probably cry. George would get red in the eyes and lose his voice for a moment or two, and then he'd pull her into his arms and whisper something sweet, like, "Girl after my own heart." They would want to know how she did it, and when she told them about all the hours she worked late into the night, all of the sacrifice

248

and risk and trial and error, they would shake their heads in amazement. Sadie would whisper, "We had no idea." And Jessie would feel like they loved her and were proud of her and all of her achievements.

Jessie had sworn off champagne, so she was chilling a bottle of sparkling cider. She didn't set out the glasses, though. Not just yet. She wanted the celebration to be a surprise.

She finished the salad and glanced at the clock. Six fifteen. They were late, but no problem. She sat down with her new ebook, but she couldn't focus. She glanced at the clock after every page and at the rumble of each car that drove past. Six twenty. Six thirty. At six thirty-six, the phone rang.

Jessie sprinted to the receiver, thinking that the only thing that would make the night better would be Nate. Maybe he was calling. "Hello?"

"Hi, honey," her mother sighed on the other end. "How are you doing?"

Her throat constricted. "I'm okay. Are you on your way?"

"Well, that's why I'm calling. Your father is traveling in the morning, and so we were thinking that we'd make this dinner another night, if that's okay with you."

Jessie looked at the giant salad bowl on the counter, filled to the brim with more kale than she could ever possibly consume. She felt the anger bubbling, and tried to swallow it down. "I already made dinner."

"I'm sure you can have the leftovers," Sadie said brightly. "Your father will be back by Saturday. We can reschedule then, if that's all right."

Jessie gripped the receiver in her hands, squeezing until it hurt. "It's not all right with me," she said. "You're almost forty minutes late, and this is very inconsiderate."

There was a long stretch of silence before Sadie said, "I thought I explained what was going on. Your father is tired, and he has a business trip —"

"Why don't you ever want to see me?" Jessie's voice broke. "Why don't you ever make the effort?"

She looked at the salad and the plate of chocolates, and at the little table that she'd set up outside on the patio. She thought of the cider in the refrigerator and of all the things her parents were supposed to have said to her that evening and now wouldn't. But she was too angry to cry. "This really sucks, Mom."

Sadie sighed into the phone. "I guess I don't see what you're so upset about. I thought we were just having dinner."

It wasn't just dinner. It was the Big Fix. The moment when everything would be better between them: all of the hurt and resentment would dissolve, and from that point forward, Sadie and George would want to be her parents because they would see her as a child to be proud of. They would be sorry they'd been so absent and missed so much time with her. A kale salad and some chocolate would change everything.

She bit her lower lip to stop it from trembling. "Tell Dad to have a good trip," she said.

"I will. He's going to Seattle, and you know he loves it there."

Sadie continued, but Jessie wasn't listening. They disconnected the call after making a vague promise to reschedule. Jessie had lost her appetite. She took the chilled cider out of the refrigerator and put it in a small paper bag. Then she left the house.

Uncle Hank was still working. She knew he would be. But she didn't want to bother him, so Jessie took a seat on the wooden staircase behind the bakery. The white paint was chipping and worn in a familiar pattern. Sometimes she missed living there.

She uncorked the apple cider and held the bottle away while it spilled out of the top. Then she took a sip, staring out into the back parking lot. It was quiet there, and hidden. Jessie enjoyed the silence until a few minutes later when Uncle Hank poked his head out of the back door. She'd known he would. "I thought I heard someone on the back steps," he said. "What are you doing, honey?"

She held up the bottle. "Drinking sparkling cider out of a paper bag. Want to join me?"

He smiled, wrinkling the corners of his eyes. "Love to."

Uncle Hank was still wearing a plain red apron as he stepped outside. The wooden stairs creaked under the weight of his steps. Jessie scooted over to one side, and he took a seat one step below her. "Everything okay?"

"No." She crinkled the bag in her hands. "I was supposed to have dinner with Mom and Dad, and they just cancelled on me." She paused. "They always do that. Ergo, the cider."

Uncle Hank was quiet. He rested his arms across his legs and leaned his head back against the railing. Jessie took another swig of cider. "I don't know why I expect more," she said. "From them, or from other people. I sometimes think that if I were only a little better, things could be different. If *I* were different, they would love me."

Gosh, did it hurt to say those words. Uncle Hank's forehead creased and he said, "Can I tell you something that I should've told you a long time ago?"

Jessie leaned back. "Sure, why not?"

"Years ago, when your dad told me that he wanted me to watch you while they were in Germany, I was speechless," he said. "I was angry at first, thinking that I had this bakery and my own child to worry about. I'd just gone through a divorce, and it's not like we had lots of extra room in the apartment." He shifted to set his elbow on the stair behind him. "Your dad told me how much he'd be traveling, and how he wanted you to have some stability through high school. When he put it that way, I didn't think I had a choice."

Jessie chuckled mirthlessly. "Dad's good at selling people things."

"That may be," Hank agreed. "He's my little brother, and I guess I've always helped him out through the years. I thought I'd be doing him a favor. But then you came to live with us, and you fit with our family perfectly. You and Wren — you became like sisters. Best friends."

Jessie's throat tightened as she thought about how much she missed that time, when she and Wren could lie awake in their beds and talk late into the night. Being an adult was so lonely. "Thanks, Uncle Hank."

"I'm not finished yet," he said, and patted her on the leg. "Jess, I know how much of yourself you give to others, and I know how much people can disappoint you. But I hope you know how hard I've tried not to let you down. The minute you came through that door" — he pointed to the apartment door above them — "I wanted to create a home for you here. I don't think of you like a daughter. In my mind, you *are* my daughter. You complete our family. And I couldn't be more proud of who you are."

Jessie blinked back her tears and leaned forward to throw her arms around her uncle. "Thanks," she murmured against his neck, inhaling his familiar scent of Ivory soap, flour, and sugar. "I've always felt like this bakery was my real home."

"You don't have to thank me. I should've told you all of this long ago." He wrapped his arms around her and hugged her tightly. "Look, people are who they are, and you are who you are. Please don't change. I happen to think you're pretty great."

Jessie gave him one more squeeze before sitting back again. Her thoughts suddenly flew to Nate, and how angry she'd been when she'd learned that he'd rented the space she wanted. People like Nate were hard to find, and

253

she'd lost sight of what was important. "I haven't been fair to someone close to me," she said. "There was this misunderstanding, and I feel pretty bad about it."

"So what do you think you're going to do?"

Jessie reached for her bag of cider and cradled it in her lap as she thought. Nate had signed a lease, and the Dinardo space was gone. No sense getting upset over it now. But there *had* to be another option, if only she could think of it —

Then suddenly, it hit her. Maybe she'd known it all along. Maybe that's why she'd come to the bakery that evening. She looked at her uncle. "Uncle Hank. I just had a brilliant idea."

He lifted his eyebrows expectantly. "I'm all ears."

She paused while she thought it through. The more she thought, the more her heart raced. Yes, this could be perfect.

Jessie grinned. "Okay, first tell me: how do you feel about polka dots?"

CHAPTER SEVENTEEN

NATE COULDN'T BRING himself to look at the lease. He kept it tucked between the seats of the SUV. He had a list of things he needed to do to get his business going, a series of menial and significant tasks. He tackled a few and tried to pretend that he didn't feel rotten.

The things he'd said to Jessie — he'd had no business. He shouldn't have spoken to someone he loved that way. But when he'd seen the disappointment in her eyes and known that he'd hurt her, he'd lost control. Big time. And knowing Jessie and how sensitive she was, there was little possibility of repairing the damage.

A few days after the argument, Quinn appeared at his doorstep. He had his hands tucked in his pockets, and he looked nervous. He was sober for a change. "Hey," he said.

"Hey," Nate replied. There was a pause before he added, "Do you want to come in?"

"Sure."

They sat on Nate's couch and talked about everything else: the weather, the ball game, and plans for the upcoming weekend. Finally, Quinn said, "I'm getting sober. My life is...not what I want it to be. I've hurt you, and I've hurt Caryn. And Jessie, of course. I don't recognize who I am sometimes. I want to get better."

Nate's shoulders relaxed. "I support you."

"I knew you would." Quinn shifted, and he crossed his ankle over his knee. "I want to apologize to you, because what I said about Jessie, and implying that she was flirting with me...that was really shitty. And it wasn't true. She completely told me off, and I guess I was pissed." He raked his fingers through his hair. "Caryn told me I have a drinking problem. I think it's true. Anyway, I needed to apologize to you because I'm an ass. But you know, you're wrong when you say that I think I'm better than you. You've always been my best friend. It's just that I've been screwing that up lately."

Nate's throat felt tight. In all the years he'd known Quinn, he'd never heard this kind of apology. It was the best thing he could remember ever happening between them. He held out his hand. "I'm here for you. Always."

Quinn accepted the handshake and embraced him. "Thanks, man."

They didn't talk for long before Quinn excused himself and mentioned he had a meeting to attend. Nate closed the door behind him and stood for a few minutes in the kitchen, alone with his thoughts. Quinn had always been brave. It had taken guts to come over and apologize. Nate had been an ass, too — to Jessie. Deep down, he knew he was only making excuses when he told himself that Jessie wouldn't forgive him. It wasn't about him being forgiven. It was about righting a wrong.

As he grabbed his jacket and left his house, Nate knew where he was going, but he didn't know what he'd do when he got there. He smiled as he thought about Jessie saying that she often turned off her brain while her mouth was running. Didn't that mean that her words must have been coming from the heart? Not enough people opened themselves up that way. He loved her for that.

He loved her, period. And she needed to know it.

Jessie was alone when she heard the knock. She thought maybe Wren had come over. But when she opened the door, she saw Nate. Standing there. Staring at her like a lost puppy.

"Hi," he said.

"Hi." She kept a hand on the door, not knowing how she should respond. "Did you come to get your things?"

"No. I don't care about that." He shoved his hands into the pockets of his jacket. "I came to talk to you."

Her fingers tightened on the door. "It's late," she said, even though it was barely nine. "I have to get up early."

"I know. I don't want to take your time. Not too much of it, anyway." His green eyes searched her face. "I have two things to say. One, I'm sorry. I said some terrible things to you, and I was wrong. You don't need to forgive me tonight, but I hope you will think about it and forgive me some day."

Jessie swallowed and nodded. "It's okay."

"No," he said, inching forward. "It isn't." He paused. "Do you remember that summer when you were working at Madame Rousseau's as a psychic? And I stopped by and you gave me that reading?"

Despite herself, a small laugh escaped Jessie's lips. She'd taken the job reluctantly, manning the crystal ball on Tuesday and Thursday nights so Madame Rousseau could take her kids to swimming lessons. "Yes. You had twenty dollars to burn. You told me to tell you something profound about your life. And I said —"

"And you said that the spirits didn't take orders. And then you told me that I was destined to have a tragic love affair that would change me forever."

"I'd been reading *The Great Gatsby*," she said. "It was assigned reading for senior year English —"

"And I knew you were making it up as you went along," he said, coming closer. He gently lifted her hand and held it in both of his. "But I fell completely in love with you that night. With your energy and your humor. I loved that you put your entire heart into giving out fake psychic readings, and all these years later, I still see you giving your heart to everything you do."

Darn it, that had caught her by the feels. Her eyes began to sting. "I don't know what to say," she whispered. "Thank you."

"For loving you? I hope you know how easy that is." He brought her hand to his lips. "I also hope that you know how sincere I am. I love you, Jessie. I've messed everything up, and I'm a complete jerk, and I still love you. And if I thwart a million more of your business plans inadvertently, I will love you. Because I can't imagine a day when I wouldn't want to share everything that happened with you, or an evening when I didn't think of you as the brightest star in my sky."

That did it. She was crying. "I missed you." She threw her arms around his neck, melting against him. They were perfect together — a foregone conclusion. She may have spent the last few days standing on her own two feet, but life felt so much better with Nate in it. "I love you so much," she whispered. "Please don't go again. Not even when I tell you to."

"I promise," he said, and pulled her tighter against him. After a moment, he released her and took a half-step back. "Look, about the space —"

"It's yours. I want you to have it. I have it all figured out," she said. She couldn't stop smiling if she tried. "You know the empty apartment above Hedda's? I'm going to convert it to a large kitchen and a small retail space. Most of my business doesn't come from foot traffic, anyway. Plus, I love working with Uncle Hank and Emily. I'll be happier being close to them." That bakery was home, and she didn't want to leave it.

Nate's face brightened. "And Uncle Hank is fine with that?"

"He's thrilled! He loves the idea of converting it. He never wanted to be a residential landlord, anyway. The best part? He's waiving the rent. He'll be a partner instead, and he'll help me with some of my start-up costs."

"Wow. It's perfect." He shook his head. "I don't know what to say. You've clearly been busy for the last few days."

"You don't know the half of it," she laughed. "I ordered three sets of knives!"

"Wait...what?"

"I'm so happy you're here." She laced his fingers with her own. "You have to come inside. I've been dying to tell you everything."

EPILOGUE

CONSTRUCTION ON THE old apartment above Hedda's took a little longer than expected, but it was coming along, and Jessie expected to open her chocolate shop by September. There would be a pink and white polka-dotted awning, of course, and white scroll on the windows: Sweet Possibilities. "I considered 'The Chocolate Crush,'" Jessie would explain when asked, "but it sounds kind of violent."

While she waited for her shop to be finished, Jessie spent nearly all of her work hours — and long hours afterward — fulfilling orders for a number of large retail clients. They'd found her from word of mouth after the "Sweet Relief 5K"...which she and Nate had completed side by side, though hardly in record time. It didn't matter. They agreed they'd do it again, and they felt good knowing they'd helped to purchase a new roof for the food shelf.

Nate's venture — Cove Fitness — opened in early August to a stream of eager clients. He'd hired staff in advance, but he scrambled to find more personal trainers to meet the demand. He was successful beyond his wildest dreams, but it came as no surprise to Claire. Or to Jessie.

As for Wren and Jax, they may have worked in showbiz, but there was no drama at the altar. Wren looked stunning in a white chiffon gown and a veil that trailed elegantly behind her as Uncle Hank walked her down the aisle. Jax mostly minded his manners, though he did strip down to his boxers and jump in the infinity pool toward the end of the reception. And Jessie's dress fit. Like the proverbial glove, actually. In all the years she lived, she would never forget the look on Nate's face when he first saw her in it.

"You can't wear that," he said. "You'll upstage the bride."

"Yeah, right," she said. "You remember my cousin Wren, right? The tall, gorgeous one?"

Nate pulled her into his arms. "In case you haven't noticed, I tend to not notice things like other women when you're around. With that dress, you may as well have put blinders on me."

Jessie loved living with Nate in the little cottage. He was probably the only man in the world who wouldn't insist on stuffing Prince Travis in a plastic bag filled with mothballs and hiding him in the attic. Also, after only a week of living with beige walls, Nate had agreed that Jessie could add some color to the space. He'd even helped her to paint the living room a bluish-green with white trim.

Oh, and she'd finished *To Thrill a Cockingbird*. She'd even shared some of the passages with Nate, though she'd discovered that he couldn't focus on the text for very long. He quickly became preoccupied with trying to get her into bed. Not that she minded.

All in all, even though Jessie decided it was the best summer she'd ever had, she knew that things would only get sweeter.

And to think that all of it had come from drinking too many mimosas.

* * * * *

A Note from the Author

THANK YOU FOR taking the time to read A SWEET POSSIBILITY! Reviews help readers to find books they will enjoy. If you are so inclined, an honest review at the site of your choice would be appreciated.

If you would like to be the first to know about discounts, special events, and new books, please visit my website at nataliecharlesromance.com and sign up for my newsletter. And if you would like to contact me directly, please email me at writernataliecharles@gmail.com.

Finally, I would like to thank the many amazing people who comprise my writing support system and made this book possible. To my insightful beta readers, my eagle-eyed editor Amanda Sumner, and the ever-understanding Mr. Charles: thank you, from the bottom of my heart.

About the Author

NATALIE CHARLES HAS worked as an attorney, a playground supervisor, and a makeup sales clerk, but not in that order. The happy sufferer of a lifelong addiction to mystery novels, Natalie has, sadly, never out-sleuthed a detective. She is a RT Reviewer's Choice Award winner and has been a finalist for the Daphne du Maurier Award for Mystery/Suspense. She lives in Connecticut with her hero husband and two bookish children.

Natalie loves connecting with readers! You can find her on Facebook, facebook.com/writernataliecharles or Twitter @tallie_charles, or you can contact her through her website, nataliecharlesromance.com; or email at writernataliecharles@gmail.com.